C000133563

THE
BIG
BLIND

THE BIG BLIND

LAVIE TIDHAR

2020

The Big Blind
Copyright © 2020 Lavie Tidhar

The right of Lavie Tidhar to be identified as Author of this Work
has been asserted by him in accordance with the
Copyright, Designs and Patents Act 1988.

Published in October 2020 by PS Publishing Ltd
by arrangement with the author.
All rights reserved by the author.

FIRST PS EDITION

ISBN
978-1-78636-599-6 (Signed edition)
978-1-78636-598-9 (Unsigned edition)

This book is a work of fiction. Names, characters, places and incidents
either are products of the author's imagination or are used fictitiously.
Any resemblance to actual events or locales or persons, living or dead,
is entirely coincidental.

Cover and book design by Pedro Marques.
Text and titles set in Caslon.

Printed in England by the T.J. Books Limited
on Vancouver Cream Bookwove 80 gsm stock.

PS Publishing Ltd
Grosvenor House
1 New Road
Hornsea, HU18 1PG
England
editor@pspublishing.co.uk
Visit our website at **www.pspublishing.co.uk**

I

CLAIRE SAID, 'Raise.'

She stacked chips. One pile, two, three. Started again. Not looking at the cards, not quite looking at the other players. Not not looking, either.

It was quiet in the small poker room at the back of the Dales. The sound of chips, the snap of cards on the felt. Cigarette smoke in the air, and someone coughed, someone else said, 'One time, just one time,' softly at another table.

Claire pushed the chips in, with a sort of careless studied gesture. They toppled across into the pot. It was a large pot.

The player on her left said, 'All in,' and pushed the remainder of his chips in. Immediately. But she'd expected him to do that. He had a short stack.

The rest folded, one after the other, until it came to the Docker. He was a short man and now running to fat but there was muscle under there. They said he used to work the docks. They said he did time in an English prison. They said all kinds of things. He looked at her. She looked nowhere, trying not to give anything away.

You never played the cards, as the old saying went, you played the players.

He took his time, but that was all right. He had a big decision to make.

She wished he'd get it over with, though.

'A flush?'

Someone else said, 'Only one way to find out.' Someone else laughed, but quietly. The Docker shrugged and folded.

She turned over her cards and the short stack did likewise. The river was a three of hearts and she didn't make the flush but her two pair still beat the short stack's. He got up to leave the table.

'Nice hand.'

She shrugged. The dealer shuffled the cards and dealt and round the table they went again.

4

There were three of them left after another hour. Her and the Docker and some kid, kind of cocky, with black curls of hair. He flashed her a grin. Nice teeth, and he knew it. He bet. She called, wanting to see the turn.

When the turn came it didn't come her way but she had position and she used it, applying pressure, and the kid folded.

'Hey,' he said, 'what's your name?'

'Claire.'

'I'm Mikey.'

'All right.'

He smiled again. He had an easy smile.

'You're good,' he said.

'I know.'

Even the Docker smiled at that. The next round he raised pre-flop, she folded, and the kid called. She took a sip of mineral water, watching the play. A raise and a call on the flop. She couldn't read either of them.

On the turn the kid went all in. Quick call from the Docker. He turned his cards over.

A full house. A look of disgust in the kid's eyes. Turned his own over. It was a lower full house.

River came. It was a deuce of spades, no good to anyone. The kid got up.

'Good hand.'

'Yeah,' the Docker said.

'Mikey.' The kid was looking her way again. Wore a new smile, like he had no care in the world. She thought maybe he didn't.

'Excuse me?'

'Just in case you forgot. I'll be seeing you?'

'Why not, long as your money's good at the table.'

The kid laughed. Then he went over to the bar and got himself a beer.

A few rounds later the Docker went all in on a semi-bluff and she called with a three of a kind but he got lucky on the river and with that the game was over. She collected her second-place winnings from Peg, the cashier.

'How's your dad, Claire? He's not been round these parts for a while.'

'He passed. Last year.'

'I didn't know. I'm sorry. Was it . . .'?'

'It was cancer. It was . . . It was pretty quick.'

Peg touched her hand, lightly. 'I'm sorry.'

'Thank you.'

'He was a character, was your dad.'

'Yeah.' She tried to smile. 'He was.'

She took the money and turned to leave. Went past the kid, Mikey, necking a bottle of beer. Gave him a nod as she stepped out into the night, cold air, the smell of rain.

She pulled her coat around her and stepped into the drizzle.

❊

She had to wait at the bus station for over an hour. She got a coffee and when she'd finished it she went into the bathrooms and changed into her habit.

❊

The ride back was quiet. Her head rested against the window. It was another hour on the bus and dawn was just beginning to break on the horizon when they got to her stop. She got off.

There was no one around and the convent was quiet. She climbed over the wall and got in and went into the chapel and put the envelope with the money into the collection box and then she went up to her room. She lay on the bed, staring up at the ceiling, and fell asleep for an hour before waking up again for Vigils.

2

'RAISE, FIVE HUNDRED,' Sister Bertha said. She pushed three red-topped matches and four burnt matches across the table into the pot. It was after Compline and the three of them were playing cards on the low table in Sister Bertha's room.

Sister Mary looked at her, frowned, and folded.

'Re-raise,' Claire said. 'Two thousand.' She pushed across twenty matches, none of them burnt. Each was worth one hundred. Sister Bertha glared at her.

'You're bluffing.'

'Only one way to find out.'

'You think you can push me around, Claire?'

Claire shrugged. Sister Bertha drummed her fingers on the tabletop.

'You're bluffing,' she said again.

Claire kept her face impassive. It didn't do to underestimate Sister Bertha. Her play was aggressive and she was fearless. If she had anything, she'd call without qualms.

The question was: Did she have anything?

'Why the big raise? Are you trying to push me off the pot?'

Nothing.

'You have queens?'

Bertha had an uncanny ability to read the table.

'Cowboys?'

Claire said nothing.

'What do you have that could beat me?'

The longer they talked, the more likely they were to fold. Bertha was just trying to talk herself out of calling.

'Oh, heck,' Bertha said, and folded, at last. Claire turned over one card, and it was the Queen of Spades. She mucked the other one and smiled at the older woman.

'Oh, heck,' Bertha said. She took the cards and began to shuffle.

'Mary, you're the small blind,' she said.

'I'm almost out of matches,' Sister Mary said.

'Chips.'

'I mean, chips.'

She had a quiet way of talking. She posted the small blind, two black matches. She only had one red match left.

'Well, you're still in the game,' Sister Bertha said. 'All you ever need is a chip and a chair.'

'Where did you learn to play?' Sister Mary asked.

'Back room of my daddy's pub.'

'You play so well.'

'Not as well as her,' Sister Bertha said, and pointed her thumb at Claire. 'I can play for matches. She can play for God.'

'Do you think it's wrong?' Claire said. She said it quietly. Sister Bertha was laying down cards.

'What?'

'Do you think it's wrong? To gamble?'

'Gambling is not a sin, child. Avarice is. Do you play for the love of money, Claire?'

'No. But I . . .'

'You'd play if there was no money involved. You'd play for matches. You play because God's given you a talent, and you use it.' Sister Bertha smiled as she watched Sister Mary pick up her cards. 'And besides, if poker really *was* just a game of luck, even Mary here might win a hand every now then. Raise, one thousand.'

'I fold,' Sister Mary said meekly.

3

CLAIRE CHOPPED ONIONS. She added them to the big pot. The onions sizzled as they hit the hot oil. Made her think about her father, coming back from a late-night session, walking in. He'd smelled of sweat and cigarettes and aftershave. He always dressed well for the games. Didn't matter where the game was. A rich man's home or a caravan park, the back room of a pub or the Legion. He always dressed the part and he often carried a gun. Back then, poker was illegal, and more than once he'd had to defend his winnings. When he'd come home he'd take off his jacket and roll up his sleeves and go into the small kitchen and cook. The smell would often wake her up. Fried onions, sausages. He'd sit at the kitchen table and eat his meal and she'd come in and get a hug, and sometimes they played a hand or two while he ate. Her father was never far from a pack of cards.

'What am I supposed to do with these cuts?' Sister Mary said.

The man from the chicken factory shrugged. 'Beggars can't be choosers, Sister,' he said.

Sister Mary held up a hairless wing dangling between her fingers. Even from where she was standing, Claire could see the sheen of perspiration on the skin of the chicken.

'Well?'

'It's not expired,' the man said. He was more defensive, now. 'It's fine to cook.'

'And anyway it's nothing but skin and bones.'

'Look, sister, what do you think I can do, here?'

'Show compassion for the needy.'

The man shrugged, defeated. It was hard to argue with a nun. 'It's not up to me,' he said tiredly.

When he was gone Claire helped Mary move the boxes. The smell of the chicken cuts wasn't particularly pleasant. She and Mary did their best cleaning up the pieces—wings, necks, giblets. Claire added the wings into the pot and stirred them round. The necks they could use for soup. She added stock and potatoes and carrots that had come in from a donation the day before. They were lumpy, and had taken forever to clean and peel, but they would do.

It was warm in the little kitchen. Beyond the counter the regulars were already assembling. The television was on with the sound down low and a daytime talk show where people shouted at each other. Claire left the pot to boil and helped make tea. People always wanted tea. The town had been prosperous once, long ago, but with the mines all closed and only the chicken factory on the edge of town running, it was hard to make ends meet.

'I don't know what to do,' Sister Mary said.

'It can't be that bad,' Claire said.

'It is,' Sister Mary said; but she said it quietly.

✸

They served lunch and everyone was very orderly and Marybeth Ryan came in with her new baby and everybody gathered round to coo at him. It was a little boy. When everyone'd finished and left home for the day, Claire and Mary cleaned up and Claire looked at all the tiny bones that were left on the plates.

It was hard work but it was satisfying, and she knew they helped people. When they finished they walked back to the convent, which lay on the outskirts of the town. She looked at the old building and she knew how rundown it was, and how the roof needed repairing, and how cold it got in the winter with drafts coming in and mould growing in the corners from the humidity. After Compline she went back to her room and lay down. She read a little from her book—Doyle Brunson's *Super System*, an old favourite—but then she put it down and she fell asleep almost immediately.

4

'I WAS PLAYING THIS KID last night over at
the Victoria, I raised with nothing, deuce eight
off-suit, kid called, I got trip eights on the flop.
Kid raised me, I raised him all-in, he called.
Next thing you know I'm busted out when he
made his flush. Just my luck, right?'

He looked at Claire as though expecting a
reply.

'So?' she said.

'So it wasn't any fun.'

He raised and she called.

'I didn't see you there,' he said.

'So?'

He gave her a grin. 'So if I did, it might
have been more fun.'

Another night, another game. She paired

her jack on the turn. Mikey was slow-playing his cards. Claire paired her queen on the river. She pushed a big bet. Mikey looked at her ruefully and folded.

'Maybe not that much fun,' he said, and she laughed.

She played tight for the next few hands. Mostly sitting them out. The cards weren't going her way and she didn't feel like mixing it up. This wasn't an elimination tournament, it was a cash game. Patience paid.

'Are you going to London?' Mikey said.

She looked his way at the apparent non sequitur. 'Excuse me?'

'London,' he said, drawing out the name.

'What's in London?' she said.

'The EPC,' he said. 'The European Poker Championship.'

'Oh,' Claire said. 'No, I don't think I am.'

'Why not?'

'Excuse me?'

'I said, why not? You're good.'

'I don't—' she almost checked her cards then, even though she'd just folded. She gave him back a look, the sort that said *Are you for real?*

'What's your deal, Claire? I can't figure you out.'

'Are *you* going?' she said.

'It's a five grand buy-in,' he said.

'I don't have five grand,' she said, and felt strangely relieved. So that's that, she thought.

Mikey said, 'There's a satellite tournament in Dublin. If you win there, you win a seat at the EPC.'

'Think you can do it?'

'I know I can,' he said. 'I know you can do it, too.'

'Well,' Claire said. 'I'm not.' She pushed her chair back and collected her chips. Less than she'd hoped, but she'd just been grinding it tonight. 'I'll see you.'

He caught up with her as she was cashing out. 'The satellite's next week,' he said. 'I'm going to drive. You could come with me.'

'I won't.'

'What are you going to do?' he said, sounding genuinely exasperated. 'Keep playing old men in dingy pubs for pocket money? You can *play*. You've got talent.'

'It's just a game,' she said.

'No!' he said. 'No, it's not just a game, and you know it isn't. I know you do, I can see it, the way you look at a player when they make a play, the way you study them. I can see the way only the tips of your fingers touch the cards, and how you don't give anything away, and how your mind works when you're figuring out the odds. For you, for me—it's *the* game, Claire! There's no other like it.'

'Look,' she said. He was making her angry. She wanted to push him. The Claire she'd been, before she heard the call . . . that Claire would have hit him. She used to run rough in the old days. Drink and smoke and get in trouble. She still knew how to boost a car. 'Look, just leave me alone.'

'All right.' He took a step back from her and for just a moment he looked older. 'But I'm going in three days, leaving early. I like it when it's just before dawn. When the whole world's quiet, and everyone's still asleep.'

'A poker player morning.'

He laughed. 'I'll wait at the tea hut by the bus station for an hour,' he said. 'Just in case you change your mind.'

She knew the place. It never closed. It was where cabbies and truck drivers and police officers all came to get a bite to eat at night. It was the sort of place every poker player knew. She nodded.

'All right.'

She cashed and left. She thought about the EPC on the bus back, all the way back. She wasn't going to go. It was just a crazy dream.

5

'SO YOU'RE THE MYSTERY elf who's been leaving gifts of money in the collection box.'

Claire, caught in the dark church with the envelope of money already through the aperture, froze.

'Mother Superior,' she said. 'You startled me.'

'Now, why, I find myself wondering,' the Mother Superior said, 'is one of my novitiate nuns skulking about before dawn, and sneaking out of the convent at night—yes, Claire, I know you haven't slept in your room at all—and just where does she go, and from where does she return, with the smell of cigarettes and the city upon her and all this money in her pocket?'

'Reverend Mother, it's not what you think—'

'Claire,' the Mother Superior said, and sighed, 'I have no idea *what* to think.'

'I play cards.'

'You play cards.'

'We have no money to feed the people in the town and I know the convent's been struggling and Sister Bertha says I have a talent and I just—'

'Is that what Sister Bertha says?' There was a quiet, dangerous tone to the Mother Superior's voice.

'No, it's not like that.'

'Does she know about your ... excursions?'

'No, of course not. No one knows ... knew.'

'You play *cards?*'

'Poker. In the big town ... I only did it because I thought—'

'You wanted to help the convent.'

'Yes.'

It was very quiet in the church. The Mother Superior paced, back and forth, back and forth.

'Do you still wish to become a nun, Claire?'

'Yes, of course! I want ... more than anything—'

'This is no way to go about becoming a nun.'

'I'm sorry.'

'Nuns do not *lie*. Nuns do not *hide*. Nuns do not play *poker*, Claire!'

'I was just trying to h—'

'This convent has survived perfectly well for centuries without your *help*, Claire.'

'I didn't mean . . . I just . . . Sister Bertha said there's no shame in playing if it's not for greed, and I—'

'It seems to *me* Sister Bertha is a little too free with her opinions, Claire.'

'Yes, Reverend Mother.'

'Tell me something.'

'Yes, Reverend Mother.'

'This . . . This poker.'

'Yes, Reverend Mother?'

'Are you good?'

'What?'

'Are you *good* at it? I assume you must be, since, to be perfectly frank, your little donations are the most money this convent's seen in years.'

'Yes, Reverend Mother. I think so.'

'And you say that while gambling is, shall

we say, at *best* a grey area, which you feel your-self exempt from on account of your lack of greed—'

'Reverend Mother?'

'Do you enjoy *winning*, Claire?'

'Winning?'

'I assume you win at this game.'

'Yes, Reverend Mother.'

'You . . . You *best* your opponents.'

'Yes, Reverend Mother.'

'And do you therefore feel *pride*, Claire?'

'Reverend Mother?'

'You prove your own superiority over others. Do you take joy in it, Claire? Do you not feel that that in itself is a sin? The sin of vanity?'

'Reverend Mother, I—'

She fell silent, then. The Mother Superior looked at her, and nodded.

'Quite,' she said. Her tone softened. 'I appreciate what it is you wanted to do, Claire. But you have to choose. You can be a card player, or you can be a nun, but you can't be both. When you came to me, when you said you heard the call—I thought I saw something in you. The makings of a nun. You have a good heart and a practical head, and you need both, but there is no shame in turning back. The world, after all, is filled with women who have not taken the vows. I know you had a troubled time before you came to us—'

'I did, but Reverend Mother, I *do* feel it. The convent isn't an escape for me. The things I did, I did because I didn't know where I was, what I wanted. Then I felt it. I felt the call. I know it's real. I was wrong to deceive you. I was afraid to come to you, before. But I was just trying to help.'

'Get some rest,' the Mother Superior said. 'You have Church History in two hours.'

'Thank you.'

'I will pray on this,' the Mother Superior said.

6

'**WHAT THE** —' Mikey said. He came into the mission with Bill Hanlon, who lost one of his legs in the mines.

Claire looked up and felt herself blush. She couldn't help it. Mikey stared at her habit.

'You're a *nun?*'

'A novice,' she said. Mikey raised his arms and let them fall. She almost laughed. He looked like a gutted fish.

'Show some respect, lad,' Bill Hanlon said. He pushed himself forward on his crutches, to the counter. 'Good afternoon, Sister.'

'It's good to see you, Bob. How are you holding up?'

'Oh, you know. How long is a piece of string?'

'A *nun?*'

'Lad!' Bill Hanlon shook his head at Claire, mournfully. 'Kids today.'

'You related?'

'My nephew. He's a bum.'

'Hey!'

'Plays cards all day, say it's work. Did you ever hear anything more ludicrous?'

'Come on, Uncle Bill. I'll buy you lunch somewhere proper.'

'Watch your tongue, lad. This food's blessed by God. What's for lunch, Sister? I pray it's liver and mash again.'

'It's liver and mash again.'

'Hallelujah! See, lad? God provides.'

He pushed himself to a table and sat down, staring intently ahead.

Claire looked at Mikey.

'So?'

'No, nothing,' he said. 'I thought . . .'

She motioned him to come closer. He edged forward, looking embarrassed. 'I offered to buy him lunch in the café but he thinks I stole the money, or something.'

'Listen,' Claire said. She was speaking softly, and Mikey had to lean forward to listen, so that their heads almost touched.

'Yes?'

'This EPC thing, in London.'

'Yes?'

'How much?'

He knew what she meant, of course. A little bit of the smile came back to his lips.

'A million for the winner.'

'A million *pounds?*'

'Poker's big business, now. It will be on television, and everything.'

'*Television* poker,' Claire said, with just a hint of dismissal.

'They say anyone who's anyone's gonna be there. Negreanu, Ivey, Harman . . .'

'*Television* poker,' Claire said; but she sounded less convinced, now.

'And six hundred thousand for second place.'

'That's a lot of money.'

'It's not even about the money, though, is it. I mean, not *just* the money. It's the winning, it's getting the trophy. It's sitting down at the table with *legends*, Claire. And then getting the chance to *bluff* them.'

'With your tells?'

He laughed, but it was a nervous sound. 'I don't have any. Do I?'

It was her turn to laugh. Sister Mary came around then with the big pot and Claire had to move away and help her with it. Later, she watched Mikey and his uncle eat. Bill Hanlon saw her looking and gave her the thumbs-up. As they were leaving, Mikey came over to say goodbye.

'My offer still stands,' he said. 'Sister.'

She shook her head.

'I'll see you.'

'I don't . . . I'm not coming back,' she said. 'It was a mistake.'

Mikey's expression was hard to read. His poker face.

'God moves in mysterious ways,' he said.

7

ONE DAY, ABOUT A YEAR before she'd joined
the convent, Claire didn't go with the others to
the rooftop of the old estate, saying she had an
errand to run, though she didn't. They often sat
on the rooftop, amidst the old mattresses and
broken bicycles and discarded cans, and they'd
drink cheap ale, and smoke and watch the hazy
sun behind the clouds and over the city, which
could be very beautiful sometimes, but more
often than not all you could see were the ugly
concrete buildings and maybe a couple having a
fight inside a flat, glimpsed through a window.
It was the sort of place where people dumped
their old cars because it was cheaper that way.

That day she didn't have an errand to get to.
She just walked, without a clear destination in

mind, listening to music streaming in through her earbuds. It was cold, she had her parka drawn tight around her. She'd been up too late the night before. Everything looked both too bright and too hazy, and she almost got run over when she tried to cross the road and didn't notice the car coming. A lot of her father's old poker buddies showed up to the funeral and, later, during the wake, they'd set up a game in the living room, and as much as it annoyed her mother, she didn't tell them to stop.

She was just walking around, aimless, when she saw the church. It started to rain and she went inside. It was very quiet, with barely anyone around. She lit a candle for her father and then she went and sat on the pews, a few rows from the altar, to the side. There was a very beautiful stained glass window overhead and it diffused the murky sunlight from outside and she could hear the rain knocking against the glass.

She'd felt something, then. It wasn't something you could put in words. Just a feeling she had. For a moment it was like her father was sitting beside her, on the next pew; not saying anything, but smiling. It was just a coalescence of light and shade. But the feeling persisted. It was very peaceful, and she felt loved. She left the church smiling, and the feeling stuck with her all the way back to the house.

8

'I UNDERSTAND, YOUR GRACE,' the Mother Superior said, in tones that nevertheless made it quite clear that, if she did, then at the very least she did not agree with the pronouncement. 'But there must be something we can do.'

Claire had passed by the office and overheard the voices and some instinct made her stop. The door was slightly ajar and the Bishop and the Mother Superior were inside.

'Numbers don't lie,' the Bishop said. He had a pleasant baritone voice and she'd heard he was a good singer back in his day, in the choir, but now he sounded tired, and a little exasperated. 'And we don't have the money to spare, Reverend Mother. We're going to have to foreclose to the bank.'

'But the convent! And all our work in the town!'

'We both knew it was coming down to this,' the Bishop said, and his tone was gentler now. 'This is not a surprise to either of us.'

'I won't accept it.'

Claire could hear the Bishop pace inside.

'What do you want me to do?'

'Give us a stay of execution, something—!'

'I already have. Reverend Mother, I have no more cards up my sleeve. Everyone's struggling. Even the church.'

'How long do we have?' She sounded defeated.

'I'll see what I can do ... maybe a month.' Claire heard the sound of his footsteps, approaching the door. His shadow fell on the lit open space in between the room and the corridor, as though it were eager to escape.

She walked on and heard him step out behind her. A few more words were exchanged, but she didn't hear what they said. When the Bishop was gone Claire doubled back. She knocked on the door.

'Yes? Come in. Oh, it's you.'

'Reverend Mother.'

'What is it, Claire? I am a little busy.'

She did look busy, and tired, sitting behind her desk, glasses perched over the bridge of her nose, accounts sheets hopelessly spread before her. The pads of her fingers were smudged with blue and black ink.

Claire said, 'It's about what I was doing, the money—'

'I told you, that is no occupation for a nun.'

'But we need it, don't we? We need it, and there's this thing coming up, and I think—'

But the Mother Superior shook her head. 'God will find a way, and a nun's a nun,' she said. 'Claire, you need to decide what you want to be, and it isn't a decision I, or anyone else, can make for you. Do you understand?'

Claire nodded. She understood.

'Goodnight, Claire.'

'Goodnight, Reverend Mother.'

She left her there, to her accounts.

9

You're doing the right thing, Claire.

You're doing the wrong thing.

You're doing the right thing, but for all the wrong reasons.

You're . . .

10

SHE HAD THE SLEEP cycle of a professional
poker player or a novelist, people who were
more comfortable in a dark bar at 4 a.m. than
they were getting up for work or Matins. But
she was still young enough that her body could
take the cycle shift and she could still go entirely
without sleep if she had to. But the secret night
runs to the card room had exhausted her.

She cared about the people they helped
and she cared about serving God, and it wasn't
something you could explain, it was just something you either felt or you didn't. All she knew
was that her life was better for it, and now she
was going to throw it away.

Early dawn at the bus station, and outside the little tea hut two policemen, and a

truck driver, and one of the regular homeless guys, were standing each on their own like little islands, drinking tea or digging into bacon butties. She stood there, breathing in the cold air, traffic fumes, the smell of frying onions. In the old days she would have lit a cigarette, to keep her company. What had she called it when she spoke to Mikey? A poker player morning.

'You came.'

She turned. He stood there in the pool of light under a streetlamp. His black locks of hair looked wet, he must have scrubbed himself up in the station's restroom.

'I didn't think you would.'

'You want a cup of tea before we go?' she said. 'It's a long drive.'

'Sure.' He was still standing there, just looking at her.

'What do I call you?' he said.

'Claire.'

'Alright.' That old smile came back to him. 'Well, tea sounds nice.'

They went and stood with the others and she ordered and paid. She also bought a couple of bacon butties. She had hers with brown sauce and he had his with ketchup.

I I

THE SUN ROSE as Mikey drove. The roads were pretty quiet. The land beyond the window was very green. Occasionally they'd pass a village or a town, or cows in a field, or a castle.

'See that structure over there?' Mikey said, pointing. Claire looked out of the window, at a rounded sort of house on a hill. It looked like a big Gothic ruin.

'Yes?'

'It's a folly,' he said. 'It's decoration. They built it to look just like that.'

'So it's like a bluff,' she said, and he laughed.

'Yeah. It's an architectural bluff.'

Mikey's car was pretty old and beat up but it ran ok. They listened to the radio. They stopped at a service station and had a coffee.

'I played Donnacha O'Dea once, you know,' Mikey said.

'The Don? What was he like?'

'Took all my money.'

She laughed.

'He has a bracelet, doesn't he?' she said. She meant the World Series.

'Yeah.'

'Show it to you?'

'No.'

As they continued driving the roads became busier, and Claire rolled down the window to half-open and let the cold wind on her face.

'You ever think of going?'

'Where?'

'The World Series.'

'I guess I thought about it, before ... You know.'

'I don't really,' he said. 'I still don't get—'

'What's to get?' she said.

'A *nun?*'

'A novice nun. And I don't know if I still am, now. I ... Look, do you mind if we don't talk about it?'

'You mean the World Series?'

She had to smile.

'You want to go?' she said.

'One day. I have to. It's the dream, isn't it? The Main Event. Be up there on the wall with Ungar and Doyle. Johnny Chan. You know.'

'I guess.'

'You could do it.'

'Your faith in me is touching.'

'Got to have faith. Sister.'

'I told you,' she said, and she drew her hoodie tighter over her head. 'It's Claire.'

'Alright.'

They drove in silence for a while, listening to music on the radio, until Dublin came into view ahead.

12

'CLAIRE? Oh my God, Claire? You're home!'

'Hi, Mum.'

The hug was bone-crushing. Her mother pulled her inside. The flat smelled of frying oil, cigarettes, floor polish, her mum's perfume, and something delicious on the stove.

'What are you *doing* here? I thought you were at the . . . you know.'

'It's a long story.'

'I'm so *glad!* I knew it wouldn't last, a lass like you, in that place.' Her mother crossed herself. 'Nothing against the Church or those nuns, wonderful people, wonderful, but it's not right, not for a young person like you . . . will you be staying?'

'Is Kevin still here?'

'You know he is, honey.'

'Then no.'

'Oh, Claire. I thought we moved past this.'

Claire shrugged. She didn't want the fight but now that she was here it all felt so inevitable, like a soap on TV that she'd watched too many times. Her mother loved soaps.

'Only a few days, then,' she said.

'Can I fix you something to eat?'

'What's that smell?'

'Beef stew and dumplings.'

'I guess.'

'Come on . . .' Her mum took her hand and dragged her to the sofa. It was brown and worn. 'Sit down, sit down. I'll put the telly on.'

13

'So, what's it like? The convent?'

'Leave it alone, Kevin.'

'Don't you talk to him like that, Claire.'

'How do you want me to talk to him, Mum?'

'Show some respect.'

'It's alright, Kate.'

Something about Kevin irritated Claire beyond words. It wasn't that he was a bad guy. He had a steady job and he treated her mum well, but maybe it was just that he tried too hard. Or maybe it was just that he wasn't her dad. She got up and got her coat.

'I'm going out.'

'Claire . . .'

'It's alright, Kate.'

'When will you be back?'

'I don't know.'

'Claire, this is *my* house, you will show me *and* Kevin r—'

She slammed the door on her way out.

14

THERE WAS JUST something about being back that felt so *suffocating*. She didn't know who she was anymore, or who she was going to be. She tried to ask God but, for the moment at least, she just couldn't find an answer, so she did what she at least knew she could do well. She went to the poker room at the casino.

15

THE SATELLITE TOURNAMENT was pretty lively. There were around two hundred entries, and she was playing pretty well—she got an early all-in and doubled up and she was having a good run, steadily accumulating chips. Her dad used to play the early TV poker shows, he got in second on that Poker Pros and Celebrities Tournament back in the day, and he enjoyed the attention, being recognised by the boys down the pub and that sort of thing, but what he'd always said to her was, there's TV poker and then there's real poker, and by real poker he meant the cash games. A pro played for money, and the money was always in cash games. It took her a while to get used to tournament play, it was faster and looser, everyone wanting to double up quick or get busted. There weren't many women playing—there never were. They kept rotating the players around the tables and she ended up playing a few hands with Mikey before they got rotated out each to another table. By the end of play they were down to just over fifty players.

'Having fun?'

They were at the bar where a few of the others congregated. She stuck to water and Mikey was having a soft drink. It didn't do to drink before the next day of playing.

'You should get some sleep,' she said.

There was something in his eyes, for just a moment, then it was gone. 'Think you'll make the final table?' he said instead.

'Or win.'

He laughed. They finished their drinks and she went back to her mother's. She unlocked the door and came in quietly and tiptoed to the sofa, where her mum had left her a blanket and pillows. She curled up on the sofa, trying to calm down from the rush of the game, but she kept running poker hands in her mind. She said her prayers and tried to sleep. She missed Sister Mary and Sister Bertha and her room, and the quiet of the chapel, and the work. She missed her dad, too, but that was the sort of loss that lingered, and had been there a long time. The flat was full of his memory. She fell asleep at last, thinking about the time he took her to see the Big Game.

16

THERE IS ALWAYS a Big Game somewhere. It's never in the news, and it's never recorded in any official poker ranking or tournament winnings or any of that stuff. There's always been a Big Game and there will always be a Big Game, and a good pro always makes sure to know where to find it.

For this one, her dad took her to the bank. He had two safety deposit boxes. He'd always said, the best place to keep your money was in the bank, but not *in* the bank. In the first box he had thirty thousand pounds in cash, and in the second there was a diamond brooch he'd won in a game somewhere. They took both and went to a little shop off O'Connell and there he spoke quietly with the proprietor and the brooch was exchanged for more cash.

The Big Game that time wasn't the sort you take a gun to, but it was the sort you might want to put a tie on for. It was in one of the big houses in Ballsbridge, and she'd never seen a place like that before, it was done in a minimal style with artwork on the white walls, and big glass windows that opened onto a private garden and a heated swimming pool. The game itself was eight men, including her father. They all took it seriously. No one was drinking apart from the one guy sipping a glass of Midleton 30 Year Old. A couple of the men were smoking cigars, which she supposed was what men did. She didn't mind the smell so much. No one seemed to care she was there. She sat by her father, mostly, and watched. After a while the rhythm of the game started to make sense, she could see which player was tight, which one was betting aggressively on nothing, which one was going on tilt when he lost a big hand. Her father played the game like he played any other game. He didn't let the money distract him. The room was quiet but for the sound of the chips hitting the pot. The dealer was a professional, she was a woman in a black tailored jacket and tie, she must have been hired from the casino. Claire got the impression her father knew the dealer but then, her father knew most people in that line of work.

Her father played a couple of big pots and lost both and his stack got short for a long while, but he didn't let it faze him, he kept playing and he built it back up. When they left they were about ten grand up from when they'd started. The next morning he drove her back to the same little shop as before and they got the brooch back plus a little gold necklace for her mother, and a pair of earrings for Claire, and then they went back to the bank and put the money and the brooch back into the safety deposit boxes.

She knew it took hard work to build up a bankroll and it only took a moment to lose it, and like all players her father had gone bust more than once. Her mother hated the game and everything about it. But she guessed her mother still loved her dad, all the same.

17

IT WAS LATE AFTERNOON when the satellite started up again. There wasn't a bubble, as
such, in this one. You played for a chance at the
Big Game and that was that, you either made
the cut or you went home empty-handed. She
woke up with a headache but it was gone when
she stepped into the casino. She took her seat
next to Tuco, a grizzled old man who'd been a
friend of her father's, and knocked him out a
few hands later when he went short stacked all-
in with a pair of sevens against her ace-five. She
got an ace on the turn and that was that for
Tuco.

The field shrunk to thirty-two, then nine-
teen, the blinds going up, and up, and up. She
kept her cool, avoided going all-in, mixed her

play. She kept growing her stack. The field shrunk, a double knockout brought them down to seventeen. Then twelve, two tables left. Mikey was still in, though he had a shorter stack. He knocked out another short-stacked player and doubled up. Ten players, then nine, then eight . . .

Then there were seven, and at last they had a final table. But only the players who finished in the top four would get the comp entry to the championship in London. It felt more focused, sitting the final table—there was a large audience all around them by then, and she wasn't used to that, and it could have been a bit intimidating but she tried not to let it tilt her and just focused on the game. Number seven got knocked out and then six. Claire raised big with a five-six of hearts under the gun and it got folded to the big blind, who called. The flop came ace, queen, deuce, with two hearts. The guy on the big blind wasn't going anywhere and she stuck around and hit a heart on the river and picked up the pot against the guy's ace-queen. He got knocked out a few hands later by another player and then they were four and Mikey let out a whoop that had everyone laughing—they were in. Claire got knocked out at third place and Mikey at two, and some guy got a trophy but they didn't stick around to see him waving it around. They had their ticket to the Big Game and that was what they'd to play for.

❋

'I'm sick I didn't win, though,' Mikey said. They were at a bar away from the casino, somewhere there weren't any other players. Mikey was drinking a beer and Claire had a glass of rum and coke.

She said, 'We got what we wanted.'

'Sure, but—'

'You want the fame.'

He laughed, a little self-conscious. 'I guess so. A little bit.'

'It's vanity.'

'There's nothing wrong with being a little vain.'

'It's a sin.'

'This really bother you?'

'I don't know. I guess so.'

'Then why do *you* play?'

'For the money.'

'So greed?' he said, and he sounded disappointed. 'Isn't that a worse sin?'

'No,' she said, 'I mean, for what the money can *do*.'

'Isn't that what anyone greedy would tell themselves?' he said.

'No. I don't know!'

'This bothers you, huh?'

'I guess it does.'

'Then go back,' he said.

'I can't. Not now.'

'Look,' he said. 'What's so great about being a nun, anyway?'

'It's a calling,' she said. 'It's not something you can run away from.'

'I'm guessing you used to run away from a lot of things,' he said. She stared at him over the rim of her glass until he raised his arms in mock-surrender.

She felt reckless. They ordered more drinks. He really did have beautiful eyes, she thought, and she felt that feeling in the pit of her stomach, that sort of slow melting gold, and she shivered.

✳

Under the awnings of a shop, later. They staggered down the road and she swayed until he caught her in his arms. She pressed into him, feeling his warmth. Their faces were suddenly close together.

'Claire . . .' he said. She could hear the sudden hoarseness in his voice.

For the briefest of moments, their lips touched. Barely touching, just brushing each other. Then they pulled away.

'Claire . . .'

'I'm celibate,' she said.

'You don't have to be.'

He really did have beautiful eyes, she thought. She ran her fingers in his thick hair. Touched his cheek, for just a moment.

'I know,' she said. Then she pulled away from him and walked away. She only walked a few steps and then turned and looked at him. He stood there shaking his head, and then he laughed, and she laughed too.

'I'll walk you home,' he said.

18

'A *POKER* TOURNAMENT? You play *poker* now?'

'Mum . . .'

'No, Claire! I won't let it go. Playing at being a nun, that's one thing, I didn't want you to but I thought, she's bound to get bored of it, she's got bored of everything she's done so far, how long can it last—and I was right, too, wasn't I? Seeing as you're here and all—'

'Mum!'

'But *cards?* Baby, I *lived* with your father for years! Dodging creditors, moving from one shabby flat to the next, never knowing if tomorrow we were going to eat in the fanciest restaurant in town or not have money to pay for the milk. You don't remember any of this, do you? You were small, and anyway you always worshipped him. *He* could never do wrong in your eyes. While I fed you and cleaned you and kept you warm and kept the house—kept *his* house, so he could come home at any time of the day or night, which he treated like a hotel, all so he could go back out again to play cards. Do you know—'

And out of nowhere, there came to Claire a memory, one, it seemed to her, she had forgotten, until this moment: an evening, long ago, and she was sat in front of the television, on the sofa, while her mother cooked. There was a knock on the door, a harsh fast sound that repeated, until it seemed to her it was not at all knocking but someone *banging* on the door, demanding entry. And her mother went to open it and two men barged in, and the shorter of the two pushed her mother until she almost fell, and Claire thought her mum would go for him then but she didn't; she kept back.

'Where is he?' the bigger man demanded. Claire had got the impression her mum knew him, that he'd been around before, though she didn't remember him.

'He's not here.'

'I can see *that*.'

'What do you want, Jake?'

'You know what we want.'

'It ain't nothing to do with me.'

'This is *his* house,' the man said. 'These are *his* things.'

'You leave it alone!'

'Ain't up to me, Kate. It's more than my job's worth.'

'Don't touch that!'

But this Jake, and the other man, began looking through the house, opening and shutting drawers, looking under cushions, and in the kitchen and even the bedroom—looking for money, she knew, even then. And when they found none, they took the television, and Claire started to cry, and the big man said, 'There, there, little girl—' awkwardly, but his assistant said nothing to her at all. Together they carried the television through the door and out, and in parting, the big man said, 'And tell him if he doesn't come up with the rest by Tuesday . . .' and left the rest of the sentence unsaid.

And Claire remembered her mother crying, suddenly and without warning, and without making a sound, but covering her face with her hands so her daughter wouldn't see her. And Claire remembered going to her mother and trying to hug her, and her mother pushing her away, until she relented, and extended her arms and held Claire close to her. And she remembered the tears were hot, and they fell on her face, until she was crying too.

'Claire, are you even *listening* to me!'

And she woke. She had been packing her bag when her mother came in. And now she went up to her, Kevin watching awkwardly the whole thing, no doubt wishing he was somewhere else, and she hugged her mum, just like that time, and her mother tried to push her away, and then relented. And so they stood there like that, holding each other, and Claire realised she was just taller than her mother now; as though her mother, in the intervening years, had shrunk. And she said, 'I love you.'

'I love you too, baby. You know I do.'

'And I'm sorry. For everything.' She pulled

back, and she picked up her bag off the sofa. 'But I have to go.'

'Claire? *Claire!*'

But she was gone, the door shut softly behind her.

The next stop, she thought, would be London.

19

DAY 1.

❋

Lights ...
    Camera—
    Action.

❋

'*Welcome to the glitz and glamour of the Royal Hotel in the heart of London, and to the first ever live-televised European Poker Championship! With an entry fee of £5,000 and a whopping first place prize of a cool one* million *pounds, this is the must-be—and must-see!—event of the yea—*'

Talking heads in a booth, Donald "The Duck" McPhee and Mike "The Mouse" Markosian: a popular double act on the TV circuit, she'd seen them on countless episodes of *Late, Late Poker* and *Vegas High Stakes* and *The Circuit*. She knew they'd be up there right now waiting for the edited footage from the actual game play to start rolling and, meanwhile, record commentary on the players as they began to come in. She went up to registration and queued up with the rest and when she got her bag of chips she just stood there, for a long moment, with a stupid grin on her face, until someone told her to move it.

She hefted the bag: five thousand points in chips.

This is it, Claire, she thought.

She went into the main hall to find her table.

It rained during the ferry ride to Manchester, and it kept raining on the long bus journey to London. As the bus began to wind its way through narrow streets of grey-brick buildings, early dawn came and the rain became a sort of thin drizzle which turned at last into a mist with the consistency of runny gruel. It wasn't properly cold, it was a sort of clammy damp that couldn't quite make up its mind what sort of weather it wanted to be so had just decided to be as unpleasant as possible on general principles.

She did get to see the Houses of Parliament, in the distance. At least she thought that's what they might have been.

The satellite win only covered the Main Event entrance ticket. Claire booked into a cheap hotel off Edgware Road. It was the cheapest she could find and it still cost more than a round-the-world backpacker's special for two. It cost more than the gross domestic product of Tuvalu. It cost more than a cocktail at Rules. It cost . . . anyway it wasn't cheap.

And it was a long way to go into the money.

That was the thing about tournament play. The vast majority of players never finished in the money. Their entry fee went into the pool, and then they were knocked off, one by one by one, victims to low pairs and weak aces and bad bluffs and busted flushes. Most of these players stayed the course, keeping the dream alive, sitting for hours playing hand after hand, mucking, raising, calling, going all-in . . . busting out.

Until, at last, you hit the bubble.

Once you were in the bubble the remaining players got paid. How much you got paid depended on how deep you ran. And then when you hit the final table . . . that's when the *big* payouts began.

So all you had to do, Claire figured, was get through the field of a thousand or so of the best poker players in Europe, if not the world, all gathered together in one convenient ballroom, and you were scot free. As her father would have said, it was as easy as falling off a log.

So, it was that . . . that, or bust out half an hour into the main event and go back to Ireland with nothing but the coat on her back, and a memory of the Ballymoon Hotel and its dirty carpets, shared toilets at the end of the corridor, and the strong smell of hash lingering not entirely unpleasantly in the air. She'd seen worse, just never at the prices the Ballymoon charged. *That* part was pure London.

In any case it was only a place to put down her stuff and kip for a few hours. The rest of the time she'd be in another world.

It was a short tube ride to the Royal and when she climbed the marble steps and walked through the double doors it really was another world. It was the sort of place that had chandeliers hanging from the ceiling and carpets thicker than a boy from Cork, as her father used to say. It had a sort of slightly shabby, genteel opulence. But really all anyone cared about that day was the tournament.

The thing was, there's nothing opulent or otherworldly about even a place like the Grand Hall when you have to shove a shedload of card tables and chairs into it. With the number of registrants, it was all anyone could do to barely move between the tables, and by the time the ballroom filled up with players the air became noticeably warmer, and turned somewhat fragrant with bodily odours as the day progressed. But none of that really mattered. Not as soon as they'd dealt the first hand of cards.

'Shuffle up and . . . deal!'

✳

Suited connectors, seven-eight of hearts, out of position. She mucked. But as soon as they got dealt she felt she was herself again, and she was in control.

✳

Never play the first hand in a tournament, said Doyle Brunson. And could that man sitting hunched at the next table, a wide cowboy hat on his head, his posture as accustomed to the chair as only a professional gambler's could, really be Texas Dolly? And over there, checking her phone while listening to music on her ear buds, was that Nicola "Kicker" Sinclair, two-time EPC champion, who got her nickname when she defeated Vladimir "The Impaler" Walewski at the Berlin EPC with nothing but a queen kicker to his jack?

'They've come from all over the world, drawn to the crown jewel of the EPC tour, the London event. And, as usual, we like to take an early look at the contenders—what do you think, Mike? Anyone who catches your eye?'

'Well, Don, the last person to catch my eye was my last ex-wife, and I'm still paying that one off. But sure, there are some strong players here in the field—Jennifer "Pocket Jacks" Jackson is here—'

'That's a hand no one should ever play, Mike—'

'Well, you and I shouldn't be allowed anywhere near a card table, Don, but in Jennifer's hand, a pair of jacks may as well be quad aces every time.'

'A dangerous player, indeed, Mike.'

'Then there's the Impaler, Don. A young player—'

'Aren't they all, Mike?'

'They do seem to be getting younger and younger every year, don't they, Don? But Vladimir Walewski, a young Polish-German player, has been making a name for himself on the EPC circuit, and you remember him, of course, from last year's WSoP, where he'd made a deep run at the Main Event—'

'An impressive performance—'

'A player to watch, that's for sure. Very loose,

very aggressive, my bet is he'll either bust early or make a deep run again. I wouldn't be surprised to see him at our Final Table—'

'*We've talked about the pros, Mike, but what about the amateurs?*'

'*Well, Don, with just over a thousand entrants, there are plenty of hopefuls in this tournament, young guns and grizzled old players emerging victorious from home games all across Europe. Who's to say who will triumph, and who will fall? It's Day One of the Main Event, and if we know just one thing, it's this: everything is possible.*'

'*All you need is a chip and a chair, eh, Mike?*'

'*That's right, Don. That's r—*'

She saw Mikey, at another table, but he was in a hand.

What was incredible was just how *quickly* some of the players just went for it. Within the first twenty minutes at the table she saw two guys go all-in against each other pre-flop, ace-king against a pair of jacks. It was a classic coin toss, and the flop came seven-ten-three rainbow, a very good flop for jacks, and the turn wasn't any help either but a king came on the river and the jacks busted out. Five thousand pounds, she thought, just to play for twenty minutes. And this was going on all across the tables, players were getting up and moving on, to the side games, and the remaining players kept being shuffled around to other tables as empty ones were removed, one and then two and then three, but there were still plenty of players left. It was a massive field, and the key to surviving it was to play well and to be patient. The blinds were still low and a lot of people just kept mucking their cards, waiting for a real hand to push with, and Claire was beginning to get a sense of the other players' rhythm and the way they played, when she got moved to another table.

'Hello, Claire. Long way.'

... and found herself sitting across from the Docker.

'Docker. Didn't realise you played tournaments.'

'Don't, usually. Don't like the cameras.'

He bet, half the size of the pot. On his left, a boy in a hoodie that left nothing visible of his face but his eyes, which were themselves obscured behind dark sunglasses, looked at him sideways and folded.

'So what's changed?'

She called with her pocket sevens.

'Money,' he said.

'Money?'

'Money's bigger.'

It was a long conversation, for the Docker.

'Yeah,' she said. The flop came seven-jack-deuce, with two spades on board.

The Docker raised, twenty thousand.

She said, 'Ace-jack?' and pushed all-in.

'We seem to have an all-in situation developing in one of the outer tables, Don—ah, the Docker. An old hand from the Republic of Ireland, I believe this is his first appearance at a major tournament?'

'Indeed it is, Mike—I played with him a few times and I must say, he's a formidable opponent, though he is known to prefer cash games. Now who is the young lady—?'

The Docker stared at her. She stared back. The boy in the hoodie and scarf mumbled something.

'Excuse me?'

'I said, do you think this would make the TV?'

'Oh, hell,' the Docker said, and he folded. Claire inched her head and swept the chips to her side of the table. The kid in the scarf said, 'Nice hand,' then looked down at the felt.

'Interesting table, Don. That young player to the left of the Docker—'

'Ah, yes, of course—'

'That is the infamous Phantom, isn't it?'

'Le Phantom, indeed. They say he's only twenty-one, and already a mathematical prodigy who studied for a doctorate at the prestigious École Polytechnique, but dropped out to become a professional player. No one knows what he looks like in real life, do they, Mike?'

'I believe so, Don. Le Phantom is notorious for never revealing his face in public. I see he already has a sizeable stack in front of him—well above the tournament average. But let's get back to our featured table—'

They broke for the restrooms every ninety minutes. The men's were packed outside. The women's, in contrast, were near empty. She ran into Pocket Jacks by the sinks and for a moment they both washed their hands in silence.

'First EPC?' Pocket Jacks said.

'First anything,' Claire said.

'If I could give you some friendly advice, kid: never play with money other than your own, never be unkind off the poker table or kind when you're on it, and never, ever, slow-play pocket aces.'

'Sounds like good advice,' Claire said, drying her hands on a paper towel.

'Oh, and *Rounders* is overrated. See you inside, kid. Hope you make it to the final table.'

❋

Things started going bad when she returned to the table. It didn't look like it at first. She got a pair of kings and raised from an early position and got called, and when it went to the flop there was an ace on the board and the guy she was playing against bet like he had it. He had the chip advantage too, and she thought he could be bluffing, trying to represent an ace, and she pushed in because damn it, a pair of kings was something no one liked to throw away. It turned out the guy *didn't* have an ace, he had an inside straight draw and for some reason he kept chasing it—and he hit it on the river. She lost a big chunk of her stack on that hand and after that, try as she might, she couldn't seem to do anything to improve her position, and all the meanwhile the blinds were going up and she was being eaten up alive, losing one blind after another and she wasn't getting any cards that were worth a damn.

She saw Mikey at another table and caught his eye and he grinned. She was glad for him that he was still in the game. His stack looked healthy, too. Healthier than hers but then, at that point, anyone's stack was.

Then the devil sat down at her table.

'I . . . am . . . *Mephistopheles!*' he announced in a booming, thespian voice.

He had a pointed beard and thick black hair styled up into horns, which was most likely a wig. He wore a velvet red cape and, for some reason, a cravat.

'*Going for a moment back to the outer tables, Don, I see we have a rather colourful player—*'

'*Ah, yes, Mike, there's always one, isn't there—*'

78

'One at the very least—'

'It's hard to be more... present than our Mephistopheles, though. We can give him that—'

'An enthusiastic amateur, a former English professor and founder of that website that sold for a good few millions last year—'

'Souls R Us, Don? Just kidding. But yes, Silicon Valley's latest entrepreneur turned poker player— not a bad one, at that. How many do we have left in the field?'

'We are down to just over six hundred players, Mike, and with the blinds going up I think we're going to see the game change. It's time for the real poker now—'

'Been playing long?'

'Excuse me?'

'Not seen you around, before.'

She stared across the table at him.

'I haven't been, *around.*'

'I have. Played with them all. I eliminated Barry Greenstein in a charity tournament once with an eight-ten of hearts and he gave me a copy of his book after.'

'That's nice?' She wished he would shut up.

Most players observed table manners, not talking during a hand, but some *liked* to talk, keep up patter as a strategy to needle their opponents, put them on tilt. And she was on tilt enough as it was.

'*Ace on the River*,' Mephistopheles said.

'Bit of an obvious title,' someone else said, kid on her right. 'Anyway, doesn't he give a copy to everyone who knocks him out?'

'You talk a lot, don't you, kid?' Mephistopheles said, and the kid snorted and pushed an all-in on what was probably a bluff but no one seemed in the mood to find out so he got the small pot uncontested.

Claire was really down to the bare bones now. She was well below tournament average, and she could see players getting up and leaving their tables, one by one by one. They were dropping like flies. There was only one final table, and there would only ever be nine players sitting at it, and it was a long, long way away from where she—from where anyone—was currently sitting.

'Raise, ten thousand,' Mephistopheles said.
'Fold.'
'Fold.'

Claire stared at him with something like momentary hatred in her eyes. 'If I fold, will you show me what you had?' she said.

Mephistopheles smiled. He had good, white American teeth. 'You don't strike a deal with the devil,' he said. 'Well, miss?'

'Fold.'

'That's what I thought.'

❋

Two-six off-suit: fold.

Jack-four off: fold.

Seven-deuce.

A pair of fives, a pocket pair at last—coming in after a raise and a re-raise on her right.

Fold.

On and on it went, the relentless pummelling and punching of a bad beat, and the stack before her grew shorter and shorter.

She ran into Mikey during the next restroom break.

'Hey.'

'Hey . . .'

'Still in, then.'

'Yeah.'

'Doing alright?'

'Not really.'

'Hey,' he said. 'You're still in. That's all that matters.'

'Right,' she said. 'I'm still live, right?'

'Chip and a chair,' he said, and she had to laugh, it was so pompous but well meaning.

'How about you?'

'Doubled up early with a lucky all-in, kept at it . . . riding comfortably. Hey, did you come up against Danny Boy yet?'

'Danny Boy?'

'Danny Boy Pearson.'

'*He's* here?'

'Yeah.' Mikey's smile had a shy touch to it. 'I was sitting with him at a table for a while. I went a few hands with him, Claire. With Daniel eff-ing "Danny Boy" Pearson! He has more World Series bracelets than, I don't know . . . the Pope.'

'The Pope doesn't– oh, never mind.'

'Figure of speech, Claire.'

'It isn't really, Mikey.'

'We can agree to disagree.'

She rubbed the bridge of her nose. At that moment she wanted nothing more than to be back in her room, in the convent, and for the bells to be ringing for Lauds. She began to hate the stale odour of too many men too close together, and the constant clinking together of other people's chips, and the soft whisper of cards through the air as they landed on the felt and how ... they were all ... so ... *shit!*

'I'll see you, Mikey.'

'Yeah, you too. Hey, good luck.'

'In poker, you make your own luck,' she said, hating herself even as she said it.

He only smiled. 'But a bit of luck doesn't hurt,' he said.

✳

Tried limping into a pot with a weak ace, got raised all-in and went for it. An ace came on the turn and she doubled up, the bigger stack barely feeling the dent, but it was something, it bought her some reprieve.

The big stack on the button making a big raise when she was on the big blind holding cards weaker than a duchess's tea. She folded and lost the blind, again . . .

❋

'Well, Mike, this was an exciting Day One and no mistake! We've seen pros and talented amateurs alike battle it out and get busted, one by one. The field is now down to a mere three hundred and seventy-five players—'

'An incredible achievement any way you want to look at it, Don, against some of the best players in the world—'

'Didn't you finish in the money once, Mike?'

'Not since my third divorce, Don—'

'Well, these players still have a way to go before we hit the bubble, but it's been a tremendous day of play, and as things wrap up for the night, what's the best advice you could give the players, Mike?'

'Get some rest, stay focused—this game is very

far from over, Don. And if you're down to your last handful of chips—it's time to get lucky, and fast. Say a prayer if you have to.'

'Wise words there, Mike. To everyone at home, this has been another epis—'

※

She couldn't believe it when the tournament director called time. She emerged, blinking and disoriented, from the world of gameplay, in which the only real constants were the beats of call and raise and fold, of flop and turn and river. To find herself still alive, still in the real world, the lights dimming and the empty tables removed, and chairs scraping back, and players rising and stretching their backs and each with this long distance look in their eyes, that same sense of amazement that they were still in the game.

They gave them Ziploc bags to put their chips in, and felt-tip pens to write their names and the chip count. She looked down at her stack and suddenly laughed. She was down to a single, one-thousand-point chip.

She bagged it, anyway; of course she did. Then, finally, she got up and left the table.

20

ON THE NIGHT BEFORE her confirmation, her father took Claire to a poker game. By then she'd become a regular if unofficial presence at the poker tables, a sort of novelty act. Her father would give her fifty quid, an allowance, and she'd sit down at the table, wherever it happened to be. People would be charmed at first by the sight of a young girl playing poker, her face intense in concentration. They'd pat her head or tell her bad jokes or ask her if she needed help with her cards. The money was hers to do with as she wished. If she lost it, it stayed lost. If she earned out, the fifty went back to her dad and what was left was her pocket money. People stopped patting her head and making bad jokes as soon as they realised the kid could play, but by then, she was usually up.

When they had finished that night and walked home, they went past the church where the confirmation was to take place. She held her father's hand and the rain was only a drizzle and the yellow light from the streetlamps was smudged. She loved those late-night hours and their walks, the quiet, somewhere a dog barking, somewhere a police siren going off, somewhere the sound of a bottle rolling on pavement, but otherwise quiet, so quiet. She always felt safe, holding his hand, as though they were in their own little universe that no one else could come in to.

The church was closed, and it was unlit, the priest didn't believe in wasting electricity. There was nothing special about it, anyway. It was just a building. It was just that, for just a moment, going past, and the world was silent and the lights all smudged, and golden halos around the streetlamps, she'd felt something, and it was something she couldn't explain. Something like love.

She was tired during the confirmation the next day, and kneeling there with the other children felt uncomfortable, and the communion wafer was sickly sweet and the wine made her head swim. It wasn't what she had expected, if she had expected anything at all. They weren't really religious, they just went to church a few times a year and there were things you just *did*—baptisms and confirmations and Midnight Mass—otherwise, you only went if it was someone's wedding.

It was when he got sick that she started running wild, but it was then, too, that she started finding the church something other than it had been before, a sort of safe space, a *hallow* place, somewhere she could be herself again. And when she'd first felt the call, it had evoked a memory in her, but it was only much later that she realised it was of that night, when she walked back from that game with her father, and they walked past the church holding hands.

21

'I THINK ABOUT IT, A LOT,' she said. Earlier, she'd gone into a church she'd found and there was a confession box and behind it a tired-sounding priest, and she had said, 'Forgive me, father, for I have sinned, it had been a week since my last confession.' And then she told him the story.

'And so you decided to become a nun? I'm not sure I follow.'

'You'd be surprised how much you learn about prayer from playing poker.'

'It sounds like you're quoting something, but I don't know what it is. What is bothering you?'

'I think I made a terrible mistake. I thought I knew what I wanted, and then I think I—

you know, I think I wanted to help, but maybe it was just that I missed my old life, maybe I wasn't ready, for vows. I love—I loved—the convent. I felt like I knew who I *was*, and what I was doing, and it—*I*—had a purpose. So why, why did I go back to the game, was it really to try and help the convent, or was I doing it for myself, out of vanity, or greed?'

'People have difficult motivations,' the priest said. 'It's not a case of either-or. You could be doing things for good *and* bad reasons. But what sin have you committed? You're not a nun. You had the choice to leave. It is better for people to leave if they are not ready. You could be a good person and not be a nun, you know. I could live a good life and not be a priest.'

'I wanted to help but I think I just wanted to prove myself. And now I failed at both. The Mother Superior forbade me from going and I went. And tomorrow I'm going to bust out and I'll have nothing to show for it, and the convent will close down because they won't have the money, and the people back home, the ones who are struggling just to make ends meet as it is, they won't even have the kitchen anymore. It really isn't much, but sometimes a little is all anyone has.'

'I think you're being too hard on yourself. But if it makes you feel better, I'll tell you to say one Our Father and two Hail Marys and we'll call it quits, all right? I absolve you from your sins in the name of the Father, and of the Son, and of the Holy Spirit. Go in peace.'

'Thank you, Father.'

22

SHE STAYED IN THE CHURCH for a long time. She sat on a pew and she said her prayers. A great bone-weary tiredness enveloped her. Her body felt like a great bell that had been struck repeatedly, so that it vibrated now with tiny thrums of tension. And in her mind there were all the hands she'd played, pot odds and player behaviour and what she could have done, what she could have done differently . . .

'All you need is a chip and a chair.'

It wasn't a hallucination. It was a sort of pleasant daydream, induced by the warmth inside the church and the smell of incense and the whisper of voices in prayer.

'Dad. I missed you.'

'I miss you too, kid.'

'Dad, it's all gone wrong. I don't . . .' She blinked. She felt enveloped in fog, warm, comforting. It was hard to think straight. 'Where did it all go wrong?'

'It's just a game, kid.'

'It was your *life!*'

'But that was *my* life, kid. And it didn't make your mum happy, and I hated that I couldn't be a better husband, or a better father, when it comes to that . . . I missed all your birthdays. I never saw you sing in that school play.'

'I was terrible.'

'That's kind of the point, kid.'

He smiled. He was sitting beside her now. It was the way he'd looked before the cancer, before he got so thin and gaunt and with eyes that seemed to stare into infinity. Before he'd gone to sit next to the Big Blind in the sky.

'I love you,' he said.

'I love you too, Dad.'

'You're a good person, Claire. Life is a bit like poker. You get bad beats, and then you pick up a flush on the river and you're top of the world again. I played cards because I loved cards, Claire. I loved the game, the odds, the hours, the company ... It didn't make me a good person, it was just who I was and what I chose to become. You made a choice, too. You can still follow it.'

'Is life really like poker, Dad?'

'No, of course it isn't. I told you, poker's just a g—'

'Miss? Miss!'

She blinked back tears. A figure in the haze, resolved into a stooped, apologetic-looking woman. 'We're about to close. It's very late.'

'Sorry. I'll ... Sorry.'

But when she stepped out into the night, and that slow drizzle of rain, all the streetlights wore golden halos, and all the corners looked smudged and soft and filled with their own internal glow, and she walked back to the hotel on lighter feet, and when she fell asleep, at last, her sleep was deep, and dark, and uninterrupted.

23

Day 2.

❋

Lights . . .
　　Camera—
　　Action.
　　'Shuffle up and . . . deal!'

❋

She didn't look at the cards, just said, 'All-in,' and shoved that single chip across the felt.

❋

Action around her but she won the side pot and doubled up. She lifted her eyes and looked at them, with a faint smile, and said, 'Let's do that again.'

❋

'All-in.'

Still not looking at her cards. When the river came and she had to turn them over, she was surprised to discover her pocket seven matched the river and she'd doubled up again.

❋

'All-in.'

'I'm not playing with *her*,' someone said, and folded. The next one shrugged and raised, and the rest folded, so it was just Claire and him in the pot.

'Third time lucky,' she said, and turned over her cards.

The flop came ace-deuce-eight and the turn was a queen and the river was a deuce and the guy she was playing against grunted because he was holding a pair of aces and Claire, it turned out, had a pocket deuce.

❀

'A deuce on the river never changes anything, you know, Don.'
　'It's a cold day in hell when it does, Mike.'

❀

After that she sat back and breathed. The next hand was free and she mucked it. The next hand after that she pushed on the button and took down the blinds, with no contest. And then, just like that, she was back in the game.

❀

'Nice hand,' he said.
　She looked across the table at Danny Boy Pearson.
　'Thanks.'

He smiled. He had a nice smile. He hadn't shaved, and he wore a faded T-shirt with the EPC logo on it. He looked exactly like a guy who's made twenty million dollars playing live poker, which is what he was. He looked down at his cards.

'Raise.'

She looked down at hers. He would be putting her all-in again . . . and she had an ace-king.

'Call.'

His smile grew. 'I was hoping you'd say that.'

'You want to knock me out that bad?'

'I just want to play.'

He turned over a pair of queens.

'Figures.'

Flop came three, queen, seven.

Danny Boy had three of a kind.

'Jesus,' someone said.

'Please,' Claire said, 'Don't use the Lord's name in vain.'

'What are you, some kind of a nun?'

She stared at the board. So this is it, she thought. Day 2, and she was busting out.

A jack on the turn. Suddenly she wasn't so sure.

'One time,' she said. 'Just one time.'

The dealer turned over the river and she found herself looking at a ten.

She'd made a straight—and doubled up again.

'Nice hand,' Danny Boy said, again.

❋

What you didn't understand about tournament play was how much of it you spent *not* playing. How much of it was just sitting there, hour after hour, mucking hands, waiting as other players got involved, bet, raised, called, folded, busted out, agonised over decisions that must have seemed so fundamentally important at the time but which, a moment later, became insignificant, lost to time. The blinds kept going up and the competition became fierce as they were coming closer to the bubble. And some people aggressively went all-in, trying to double up quickly or go bust, and others held on to their short stacks for dear life, trying to survive just the next big blind, and the next, just hold on to the table for just long enough to make it through the bubble, and get paid off.

But so much of it was just sitting there, watching other people play, biding your time, waiting for cards, watching the players watching the players watching the players, and trying to work out each person's range, and what they would bet and when they would try to bluff. And just trying to stay awake.

But it was coming down to the bubble and after a couple of hours of play Claire was back up, with a comfortable stack in front of her, about the tournament average, and for the first time she felt confident in where she was. The bubble was fast approaching but she had no fear of it. Players busted out and as they did more tables were carried out of the Grand Hall and now there was finally *space*, and the air felt cooler, but into this new space now came the spectators, and the camera crews, and she began to feel a new kind of nervousness, now, as the eye of the camera swept across the tables with the red light blinking and she suddenly thought,

Wait, am I going to be on *television?*

✳

'You're going to hell,' Mephistopheles said.

'I beg your pardon?'

'Hell!' He shrieked with laughter and spread out his arms like a cross. 'All-in!'

The two players between them folded. She looked at his stack. He was short.

Did she want to take him on? Mephistopheles was an amateur, and unpredictable. He could have aces, but equally he could have suited connectors or . . . nothing.

And she had him covered.

She looked at her cards, and found a pair of sixes. She figured he could have a higher pair, but she didn't think so. She figured he had two over-pairs. Ace-king, ace-queen. It would be a coin toss.

'See you there,' she said, and committed her chips.

Mephistopheles pouted. Everyone else folded back to him so he and Claire both flipped their cards over.

'A *jack-ten?*' she said.

'Hey, they're suited connectors.'

'You don't go *all-in* on suited connectors!'

'They're still over-cards,' someone else said.

'Whatever,' she said.

The dealer dealt the flop. It was a rainbow board, ace, seven, deuce.

'I like you,' Mephistopheles said unexpectedly. 'I hope you win this thing.'

'Just got to dodge a ten or a jack,' she said. 'Or I'm out.'

'One time,' Mephistopheles said. He looked very sorry for having made the bet. 'Just one time.'

The turn came, and then the river. Sooner or later, her father once said, the river must always come.

She'd dodged a ten, and she'd dodged a jack. And, suddenly, she was up with a big healthy stack.

'Good game, good game,' Mephistopheles said. He kept sitting there, for a bit. Claire swept the chips to her side and began stacking them up.

'Good game.' Then he got up and wandered off.

❋

'That was an interesting hand there, Mike. A strange all-in—'

'Not really, Don. It's eat-or-be-eaten time, and I think Mephistopheles was just trying to steal the pot. He was hoping no one had anything—'

'And in a way, they didn't. I mean, a pair of sixes, Mike?'

'A pair's a pair, at this point in the game, Don. It was an impressive call—she obviously had a good read on him and, ultimately, decided on a calculated gamble.'

'A talented young player from Ireland there, Mike—but let's go back to the Featured Table, where Danny Boy is in a hand against another young Irish player—'

❋

Then it all stopped. They played one table at a

time, one hand at a time, waiting for the next all-in raise and call—waiting for the last person to be knocked out before the bubble. In the sudden pause people checked their phones or listened to music or chatted, or went to the bathroom, or ordered a drink. Claire prayed. It wasn't about the money, or winning, or anything like that. It was just a small, private prayer, a way to express how grateful she was, for everything. The Grand Hall faded around her, the chatter and noise, until there was only her, and God, listening.

' . . . and Doug "Moonlight" Graham busts out in eighty-eighth place, with pocket aces against "Kicker" Sinclair's straight—'

Shouts, laughter, people high-fiving, cries of 'Bubble boy! Bubble boy!'

. . . and just like that, they were in the money.

❋

There was a sense, at that point, of a sort of *loosening*. The short stacks, having stuck it out that long, were finally in the money—that is, they were now guaranteed a payout if they busted—so many went all-in trying to double up quickly or bust out with the cash. As for the big stacks, they were knuckling down for the serious prize—a spot at the Final Table. This was the time for real poker, for running deep, for *making it*. A field of a thousand, shrank to eighty-seven, soon to shrink further—but there were still nine tables left, and no one was taking anything for granted.

She saw Mikey was still in. He was chatting to one of the television producers. During the break she went to the bathroom and found herself next to Jennifer "Pocket Jacks" Jackson again.

'So you're still in.'

'Guess so.'

Jackson wiped her hands on a paper towel. 'Good for you,' she said.

❋

In the cubicle when she could be alone she said

a short prayer of thanks.

Finishing in the money, even if it wasn't the big money, it was still a lot—eight grand for the next few people to bust out and then the payouts got progressively bigger. And she could give this much, at least, to the convent. It might not be life-changing money but to the people who relied on the nuns and their outreach it would be, at the very least, life sustaining.

So she said her thanks, sitting there on the loo, and then she got up, because she was going to play the best she'd ever played, and she wasn't going to get knocked out, and, 'Good for you,' she whispered, and glared for just a moment at the door to the place beyond where Jennifer Jackson had been, and then she laughed and went back to the Hall.

Where things had changed.

❋

'Claire Byrne?'
'Yes?'

It was a TV presenter, one she recognised from watching previous shows. Holding a microphone in one hand, smiling at her disarmingly.

'Could we do a quick interview?'

'For television? I don't . . .'

'Only a minute.'

She had such a nice smile. And the microphone was suddenly in Claire's face, and the lights, and the camera, and she stood there smiling stupidly, not sure what—

'Is it true you're a nun?'

'What?'

'We understand you've come here from a convent in Ireland, to—?'

'Who told you that?'

The presenter's smile hovered, stayed.

'It's true, though, right?'

'I am not a—excuse me.'

She left abruptly. The presenter's smile stayed. 'An extraordinary development,' she said brightly, 'as it turns out that, for the first time in EPC history, we have a *nun* playing the Main Event! Claire Byrne, daughter of legendary player Dave "Snake Eyes" Byrne, who passed away tragically last year. Claire, we understand, is a novice nun from a little convent in Ireland and—'

❁

Claire sat in the chair, fuming.

Mikey!

She'd seen him talking to one of the producers, but she didn't think anything of it, not then . . .

It had to be him!

She felt violated, her private life suddenly exposed on the screen. How *dare* they? she thought. It wasn't their business, it wasn't *anyone's* business!

'Miss? Follow me.'

'What?'

'You're moving tables.'

She bagged her chips, got up. Followed the producer as if in a dream. The camera followed her as she wove her way between the tables to—

'The Featured Table?'

'TV time,' the producer said, and smiled.

At registration, she'd signed a waiver form. Agreeing to appear on TV, agreeing to interviews . . .

She wasn't just going to *quit*.

She took a deep breath. She was here for a reason, a good reason. She wasn't playing for herself.

'All right,' she said. She felt the tension leave her as she sat down, Danny Boy on her right, Mikey across from her. "Kicker" Sinclair was on the big blind and a hand was in progress. She emptied her bag onto the table and began stacking chips. Mikey saw her and flashed her a grin and she ignored him. Stacking chips, one pile, then another, then another. She had a decent-sized stack and she wasn't going anywhere.

'Raise,' Mikey announced, and pushed a big bet across, casually. The hand got folded to Danny Boy, who studied Mikey for a while, thinking. Then he folded and it came to her. She was on the small blind.

'Re-raise,' she said, and she pushed half her stack across. The big blind folded quickly. Mikey stared at her with an almost wounded look in his eyes. She kept her face impassive. He studied her. The red light of the television camera blinked.

'Stop Hollywooding, Mikey,' someone said, and someone else laughed.

He kept staring at her. Kept playing with his chips. Checked his cards. She kept her face impassive.

'Clock,' someone finally said. A producer came and stood near Mikey.

'Time's been called. You have one minute to make a decision, or your hand will be mucked. Starting now.'

'What do you have?' Mikey said.

'Fifty seconds.'

His stack was shorter than hers. *Please think I'm bluffing*, she thought.

'Forty seconds.'

. . .

'Thirty seconds.'

. . .

'Twenty se—'

Mikey pushed his cards across the felt, face down, to the dealer.

Claire gathered chips.

※

'A bit of a rivalry developing at our Featured Table between the two Irish players, Mike.'

'Let's look at this next hand. Danny Boy folds under the gun. Over to our nun—'

'A nun, Don? I guess it's true what they say.'

'What do they say, Mike?'

'In poker, all you need is a chip and a prayer.'

'Don't give up your day job, Mike.'

'Claire looks down at her cards . . . She finds a pair of sevens.'

'What would you do in this position, Don?'

'I'd raise, the question is, how much.'

'Claire raises forty thousand.'

'The next two players fold to Mikey. Look at the way he's looking at Claire—'

'Sparks there. And he has an ace-king. Strong hand.'

'Does he raise?'

'He raises for sure, the question is, how much.'

'He raises one hundred thousand.'

'Everyone folds back to Claire . . . She has a decision to make, doesn't she.'

'And she calls.'

'Let's see the flop . . . oh my! An ace gives Mikey top pair, but Claire's found a seven!'

'Look at her face, you wouldn't know *what* she's thinking.'

'I bet Mikey could save himself some money if *he* knew.'

'He checks.'

'I don't like this play. I would have raised here—'

'Claire checks.'

'The turn is a king.'

'Mikey bets, fifty thousand. He's trying to induce her to call.'

'Claire's making a show of thinking about it . . .'

'She calls.'

'They're both playing a trapping game . . . you can see how Mikey is studying his opponent.'

'The river is a six, no change to anyone ...'

'Mikey raises, one hundred thousand. He thinks his aces are good ...'

'And there's the re-raise from Claire! To a quarter million ... look at Mikey's face, he knows he's beat—'

'Or does he think she's trying to bluff him? If she didn't have the nuts, that would be the only way to win the hand—'

'I think he realises she has the nuts.'

' ... and a quick fold from Mikey. With her new chip count, Claire is now on our Top Ten leader board—'

'Textbook game play from both young players—'

❋

'Good game,' Mikey said. Play was over. They were all bagging their chips. She ignored him.

'What?' he said, looking hurt.

'Nothing,' Claire said. 'Nothing at all.'

She stalked off, the bag heavy in her hands.

24

'DID YOU SEE THAT?' Sister Bertha demanded.

'What?' Sister Mary said.

'Claire!'

'What?'

'Claire!' Sister Bertha was breathing quite heavily, each word coming out like a puff of angry air. Evidently, she'd run. This in itself was remarkable.

'What about Claire? Have you heard from her? Is she all right?'

'Claire! Is on! TV!'

Sister Mary looked at Sister Bertha with concern. 'What is she doing on the TV?' she said.

'She's playing ... *poker*!'

'She's ... why would they show people playing poker on TV?' Sister Mary said.

'It's . . . are you serious?'

'I don't understand,' Sister Mary said apologetically. 'Isn't poker a bit silly?'

'Silly? *Silly?*' Sister Bertha's bellowing breaths reminded Sister Mary of the wolf knocking the little piggies' house down. 'It's a big sports show!'

'Sport?' Sister Mary said. 'How is gambling *sport?*'

'Oh, *hush!*' Sister Bertha said, looking very out of sorts.

'It's not like there's exercise involved,' Sister Mary said, with just a hint of reproach.

'Listen, you foolish woman,' Sister Bertha said, puffing up. 'I am *trying* to *tell* you, that *Claire* is on TV!'

'But what is she *doing* on TV?' Sister Mary said.

'Who's on TV?' Sister Damien, who was passing by, said.

'Claire! Claire is on TV!'

'*Our* Claire?' Sister Damien said in surprise. 'What is she doing on TV?'

Sister Bertha glared. 'Look!' she yelled.

'Claire's on TV playing poker! It's showing *right now!*'

'How do you know, anyway?' Sister Damien, who was a little old, said.

'Know what?' Sister Alatriste, who came out on hearing all the commotion, said.

'Oh for . . . !' Sister Bertha said, and she marched away. The other nuns, with a little bewilderment, followed.

❊

It was quite a sight, were you there to see it: a murmur of nuns, marching with determination through the quiet streets, black and white, black and white in the moonlight. Sister Bertha led the way, and the others followed, shaken out of their reverie by the nun's intensity, and with concern for their sister, who had gone missing. They had all liked Claire, and they were worried for her.

It was Sister Bertha, then, in the lead, and Sister Bertha who led the nuns straight to the nearest pub, a humble little establishment called the Swan. The door swung open and the nuns marched in, into a warm room scented with cider and beer. A television set flickered images high on the wall in the corner. The few solitary drinkers looked up from their pints, blinked, and at least one crossed himself while another sidled to the door and was gone, perhaps overwhelmed by the appearance of so much religious intensity in one place.

'Hello, Tommy,' Sister Bertha said.

'Sister,' the landlord said. 'What can I get you?'

'The remote control,' Sister Bertha said, with inexorable force. The landlord blinked and complied. Sister Bertha pointed the remote at the television like a weapon and pressed buttons. Channels flickered rapidly until they came to the sport. The picture resolved—a card table, people seated—

'It really *is* Claire!' Sister Damien said. 'Why is she on television!'

'Don't start that again,' Sister Bertha snapped.

'*The river is a six, no change to anyone . . .*'

'How can a river be a six?' Sister Damien said.

'*Mikey raises, one hundred thousand. He thinks his aces are good . . .* '

'*And there's the re-raise from Claire!*'

'She's trying to raise money for the convent, I knew it!' Sister Bertha said, and she clapped her hands, making the other nuns glance at her sideways. Sister Bertha's enthusiasm was practically unholy.

'But why? What do we need money for?' Sister Alatriste said. 'I thought everything was agreed with the Bishopric—'

Sister Bertha and Sister Mary looked at each other a little guiltily. Sister Damien, with a quavering voice, said that cards were immoral, and demanded a glass of sherry from the landlord. He complied, hurriedly.

'You just wait until the Mother Superior hears about t—' Sister Alatriste began, when a cool voice behind them said, 'I am astounded to find four of my nuns taking shelter at a local hostelry, Sisters. No, please, finish your sentence, dear Sister Alatriste?'

'I was just telling the sisters that I had an errand I must run, which completely escaped my mind. I really must go . . . Sister Damien, are you coming?'

'What?' Sister Damien demanded. She looked around, saw the Mother Superior, bolted down her sherry, and slid off the stool.

'Completely forgot the washing,' she said. 'I'd forget my head, next, if it weren't screwed on.' She guffawed at the landlord and followed Sister Alatriste out the door.

'Well?' the Mother Superior demanded.

'It's Claire, Reverend Mother, she—'

'I can *see* what she's doing, Sister Bertha.'

'Come on,' Sister Mary said gently, tugging on Sister Bertha's sleeve.

'But she's . . .'

'It's time to go.'

'Yes, Sister.'

On the screen, the two talking heads were discussing leader boards and hand percentages, and blinds, and ranked payouts. The Mother Superior stood her ground until the two nuns, a little sheepishly, left the pub, with Sister Bertha looking back one last time at the television, with a longing look, and one who was religiously inclined may have found in themselves a comparison to Lot's wife, looking back to Sodom for one final time.

When they were gone, at last, the Mother Superior let her shoulders sag; she took a deep breath and sat down on the stool vacated by Sister Damien.

'Hard day?' the landlord said with sympathy.

'Aren't they all, Harry?' she said.

'The usual?' he said, and without expecting a reply began to pour a half-pint glass of Murphy's. The Mother Superior watched the credits roll on the screen.

'Can you play it back?' she said.

'There's a plus-one channel, I think,' Harry, the landlord, said.

He waited for the drink to settle and then slid it across the counter. The Mother Superior nodded, and took a sip. She picked the remote and scrolled channels until the poker coverage came back on. It was just beginning.

She sat there for a while, sipping her drink.

'. . . *all you need is a chip and a prayer.*'

'*Don't give up your day job, Mike.*'

'Oh, you *silly* men,' the Mother Superior said.

25

'CLAIRE? Claire!'

She turned at the sound.

'*Mum?* What are *you* doing here?'

'My poor baby!' Her mum's hug, enveloped warmth, the smell of perfume and cigarettes.

'Oh, mum, they—'

Hurt, choking her.

'I know. I know.'

They disengaged, her mother holding her at arm's length, looking her over. The hotel lobby, or what passed for one. Shabby sofas and a television set flickering, a group of students huddled outside, smoking.

'I'm glad you're here.'

'I wasn't . . . I didn't . . . I don't want you to think I don't support you.'

'I know, Mum.'

'It's just'—she blew out a big plume of air—'a *lot* to take in, sometimes, you know?'

Claire, half-crying, half-laughing. 'I know, Mum.'

'You don't make it *easy!*'

They were both laughing.

'Being a nun was bad enough, but *poker?* You *know* how I feel about—'

'I know, Mum.'

'But I love you, Claire. And I'll support you, whatever you do.'

'Good, Mum, because I still want to be a nun.'

'A nun, playing poker,' her mother said.

'Don't *you* start.'

'I'm just *saying*.'

But she was smiling as she said it.

❋

In the room her mother started unpacking. Claire, pacing: 'Did you have to bring the content of the *entire* flat with you?'

'It's just a few necessities,' her mother said, removing shoes, shampoo, dresses, hair brushes, a robe, a hair dryer, a box of cereal. *'What?'*

'Nothing, Mum.'

'You better win this thing,' her mother said, looking around the small hotel room. The window opened up on the wall of the next building. 'You could afford better hotels.'

'I'm giving the money to the convent.'

'*Of course* you are,' her mother said.

'Mum . . .'

'I mean it. I'm proud of you.'

'Oh, Mum.'

'Come on, let me buy you a drink. You *can* still drink, can't you?'

'I'll have one, Mum. Just to keep you company.'

'*Of course* you will. Come on.'

Arm in arm, they left the room and took the creaking elevator downstairs.

The bar was lively with backpackers and students. They pressed through and her mother ordered gin and tonic and Claire had a soft drink. She hadn't really liked who she'd become, when drinking. By the time she'd joined the convent she'd stopped drinking alcohol. There was something about drink that made you want to keep *on* drinking, and she remembered one night, when she could no longer stand the atmosphere at home, her father dying in the next room, and she went out with the others, from bar to bar, drinking until they ended up under one of the bridges, a bottle of vodka, and she stood there, looking down at the cold, dark water of the Shannon, teetering on the edge, thinking how easy it would be to just . . . fall.

Then someone shouted for her, and she bent down double and threw everything up into the water, without warning, the puke burning her mouth and lips, falling . . . everyone laughed and cheered. She threw up until there was nothing left in her and then she climbed down. The bile, she thought later, tasted a lot like grief.

'Claire? You look sad.'

'I'm just remembering,' she said.

'Yes,' her mother said, and her face was soft in the dim light. She took Claire's hand in hers. 'There were good times, too.'

'Yes.'

'We had a lot of laughs, in the good times,' she said. 'I loved your father, Claire.'

'I know.'

'And he loved you. I think he would have even given up cards for you.'

'The game was his life,' Claire said.

'It doesn't have to be yours,' her mother said.

'It's not!'

'Do you really think you can win this?' her mother said.

'Yes.' She said it simply.

'I believe you.'

'Do you remember when he was on that first televised game?' Claire said. 'And we saw him on TV, and he looked so ... so handsome!'

Her mother laughed. 'Like a real movie star,' she said.

'And he said the next day, someone stopped him in the street to ask for an autograph.'

'That was just a story he made up, Claire. He was always making up stories.'

Old remembered pain in her mother's eyes. Claire squeezed her mother's hand and they both smiled.

'To tomorrow,' her mum said, raising her glass.

'To tomorrow,' Claire said.

26

Holy Mary, Mother of God,
Pray for us sinners,
Now and at the hour of our death. Amen.

❀

She woke up with a feeling that she was float-
ing on clouds. Grey daylight seeping in through
the blinds. She lay on her back and looked up,
and her lips moved in prayer. Then she got up
and put on her jeans and her trainers and her
T-shirt and hoodie, and grabbed her bag, which
was already packed, and she left.

When she got downstairs the bar was shut
but she saw a familiar figure sitting in one corner, asleep on the table with its arms crossed

and its head over its arms, and a puddle of drool pooling on the surface of the table. She went over. Shook his shoulder.

'Seamus?' she said. It was the Docker.

'Huh? What?' He raised his head, blinked against the light, grimaced.

'Oh, Claire. I busted out.'

'It happens.'

He tried to smile, failed. 'Didn't make it to the money. Was going to play the side games but met an old friend and one thing led to another.'

By "old friend" she assumed he meant the bottle, now empty, on the table beside him.

'Your daddy would be proud of you, kid.'

Some suspicion, suddenly raised in her mind. She'd been so angry with Mikey, she didn't stop to think—

'Seamus,' she said gently, 'did you speak to the TV producers, yesterday?'

'Speak to . . . ?' he said.

'Did someone ask you about me?'

'Oh!' he said. 'Yes, there was a lovely young woman in the bar near the hotel and she did keep asking me questions.'

'Did she have a camera?'

'A camera?'

'Was she one of the producers, Seamus?' she said patiently.

He blinked in confusion. 'I don't know, Claire.'

'Right.'

'Did I do something wrong, Claire?'

Claire sighed.

'It's all right, Seamus,' she said. 'It's all right.'

27

'HERE WE GO AGAIN,' Danny Boy said.

✲

'It's Day Three of the EPC, Mike, and the field is shrinking rapidly. Of the original one thousand players only twenty-seven remain in the field. We are three tables away from the Final Table and with the blinds rising, gameplay should be fast and furious as everyone has their eyes firmly on the goal—and on the one million pounds first place prize money.'

'Indeed, Don, let's take a look at our Featured Table, where grizzled pros and talented amateurs are competing against—Don, are those nuns?

✲

Claire raised her head from the cards when she heard the commotion. The cameras, which had been on her a moment before, now swung to the audience, and she could see the doors to the Grand Hall, and through the doors there marched—

'Woohoo! Claire!'

'Go Claire!'

She laughed, astonished, as the other players on the Featured Table looked on in bemusement at the nuns who came pouring into the Grand Hall. Sister Bertha was in the front, Sister Mary just behind her, and behind them came all the others, and they came until they stood just by the barrier that separated audience from players, and they cheered her on, and she was laughing, laughing and crying, the cameras watching, and she got up and went to them and hugged Sister Bertha, and Sister Mary, and for a moment she was surrounded, entirely, by nuns.

'Well, Mike, you don't see that *every day.'*

'Indeed you don't, Don. Though it reminds me, for entirely different reasons, of my fourth marriage, which—'

'Did you marry a nun, Mike?'

'No, Don, but it was shortly after that I decided to become a monk—'

'We go back to the Featured Table now, where Irish Mike—can we call him Irish Mike?'

'I think we can.'

'Where Irish Mike is in a hand against Vlad "The Impaler" Walewski—'

❋

She hadn't seen the Mother Superior.

She was back in the game, and the three tables have gone down to two. She was so close she could *taste* it.

Nicola "Kicker" Sinclair raised an all-in from an early position. Claire looked down at a pair of kings. Was it worth it? The Kicker was short-stacked. It was an easy call. Claire pushed all-in. Her bigger stack should scare off the other players.

On her left, another short stack, Billy "The Kid" Olson, looked like he was about to call, then did.

'A big hand developing on the second Featured Table, Mike, with two all-ins against our Irish nun!'

'I bet she's praying right now, Don. Let's see what we have—'

Kicker with an ace-king. Billy "The Kid" with a queen-jack suited. Claire with a sigh of relief—she was ahead, at least for now.

'The flop comes ten, eight, deuce, rainbow, Mike—'

'A good flop for kings, Don, but a straight draw for Billy The Kid gives him some outs—'

'Claire has to dodge an ace, but Kicker Sinclair is outgunned here, Mike—'

'The turn is a jack. The Kid improves to a pair, and Kicker improves to a gutshot straight draw—'

'Lots of outs for both players, but Claire's still ahead—'

'Oh, my! And the river comes, it's a king!'

'The Kid misses his straight draw, Kicker Sinclair improves to a pair of kings with an ace kicker, but Claire wins the hand with three of a kind, for a double knock-out!'

'And with that hand, we have a new chip leader, Don! An Irish nun is now top of the leaderboard, proving the old saying—'
'Please don't say it, Mike—'
'All you need, Don, is a chip and a prayer.'
'I beg you.'
'And now we have a Final Table.'

She sat there, basking in the warm glow of the victory. She saw "Kicker" Sinclair doing her exit interview for the cameras. The Kid had just got up, looking winded, and left the table without saying a word.

Chip leader, she thought.

Final Table, she thought.

There was a bathroom break. As she made her way she had to fend off newfound fans, asking for photographs. The nuns hugged her. The camera followed her for an interview.

'I'm just grateful to have made it this far,' she said, and touched her hair self-consciously. 'Excuse me.'

Her mum, with a hug. 'I'm watching. I met Sister Bertha! Your friends are nice.'

On her way to the bathroom she ran into Mikey.

'Hey.'

'Hey.'

'That was a nice hand,' he said, not really looking at her.

'Listen,' she said. 'I'm sorry.'

'What for, Claire?' His tone wasn't hostile, but it wasn't exactly friendly either.

'I owe you an apology. I thought you told them about, you know. Me.'

'I wouldn't do that.'

'I know. I was wrong to accuse you. I thought, I don't know, I thought you wanted to put me on tilt, or . . . I was wrong.'

'I want to beat you fair, Claire, or not beat you at all.'

'You'll never beat me at poker, Mikey.'

Finally he smiled. And when he looked at her his eyes were clear. He extended his hand for a shake.

'May the best player win.'

They shook. His hand was warm and dry, his grip strong. When they let go his old grin was back. 'See you at the Final Table, Sister.'

❋

Finally, the bathrooms. In the quiet of the cubicle she said her thanks. It wasn't a church but it was the only place she wasn't disturbed.

Coming out of the stall she found the Mother Superior standing by the sinks.

'Reverend Mother! I—'

'I took a later flight,' the Mother Superior said.

Claire felt tears threatening to form. 'Reverend Mother, I never meant to—'

'Hush, Sister. Here.'

The Mother Superior reached into a black bag and brought out a change of clothes. She smiled.

'Do you have time?' she said.

'But I'm not—'

'Blessed are the pure in heart, for they will see God,' the Mother Superior said.

When she came out of the bathrooms again, she wore her old habit, and the stands went wild.

'Well that's not something you see every day, Mike!'

'I . . . '

'Mike?'

'I'm sorry, Don, I think there's something in my eye.'

She took her place at the Final Table. All the other tables have been cleared from the Grand Hall, and the table stood alone in the centre, surrounded by television cameras and, beyond the barriers, the spectators.

'Claire! Claire!'

She saw Mephistopheles in his demon out-fit waving at her frantically from the stands and had to smile. 'Go, Sister!' he shouted.

'You have some curious fans,' "Pocket Jacks" Jackson said.

Claire ignored her. She looked round, at this Final Table: Pocket Jacks, Danny Boy, Mikey, Vlad "The Impaler" Walewski, Le Phantom unrecognisable behind his scarf and glasses. The rest of the players she didn't recognise.

The tournament director stepped up, microphone in hand. Short speech, Final Table, in the money, and so on—ninth place finish was worth £120,000 and fifth was £200,000, so no one wanted to get busted early from *this* table.

Then: 'Shuffle up and . . . deal!'

❂

Mikey, leading with a raise from early position. "Pocket Jacks" Jackson, countering with a re-raise. Claire looked down at pocket aces and just called. Mikey called the raise and they went to the flop.

The flop came five, four, jack, with two clubs on board. Mikey checked. Jennifer Jackson raised. Claire, stuck in the middle, felt her aces must be good, mustn't they? She flat-called again.

Mikey raised. She looked at him but he wasn't giving anything away. He could have a flush draw, she thought. He could have had a low pair and hit three of a kind on the river. Jackson called.

The turn came a six of clubs. Mikey checked. Jackson raised. Claire folded her aces. Mikey re-raised Jackson.

Jackson raised all-in, and Mikey called.

'Disciplined fold there from Claire, it's hard to give up pocket aces.'

'Mikey has the king of clubs, for a flush, and Jackson, let's see—Jackson has three of a kind, fives—she needs to pair the board on the river to beat Irish Mike.'

'Here comes the river now—it's a three of diamonds, changing nothing.'

Jennifer Jackson stood up. Mikey followed, shook her hand. She went round the table until she came to Claire. They shook hands.

'Good luck,' Jennifer Jackson said.

❋

'What do you look like without your disguise, Phantom?' Danny Boy said.

'Like everybody else,' Le Phantom said in a quiet voice. They were in a hand together. Danny Boy liked to talk when he was playing.

He made the whole thing seem like a game between friends, like just a bit of fun. But then, he'd already won and lost twenty times the first prize money. To him, this probably *was* just a day on the job.

The best players always came up tops. Poker wasn't a game of chance as much as skill, and this was evident when the same players appeared consistently in the top rankings, consistently finished in the money, consistently made final tables and won tournaments. Tournaments weren't as predictable as cash games—the large field meant that, sooner or later, you *needed* luck to survive—but the real players didn't rely on luck, they factored it into the odds and used it. A good player might lose a dozen tournaments, but the odds were such that they'd still win overall.

'I have to say, playing a nun in full habit is pretty much guaranteed to put anyone on tilt,' Danny Boy had said earlier, when he was in a hand against her. She just smiled.

'How come you *are* playing here?' he'd asked, and so she'd explained about needing the money for the convent, and about the shelter she helped run, and about the people back home.

'That's making me feel even worse,' Danny Boy had said, as he'd folded the hand. But he was smiling as he said it.

Two of the players she didn't know got knocked out, one after the other. Short stacks, they had to double up or go and they both made a stand, one with an ace-king that failed to catch against a pair of fours, and one with an unfortunate pair of kings against Danny Boy's suited connectors, which made their straight on the turn. Danny Boy's stack was the biggest on the table, but Claire's was third in size and she could afford to sit out the blinds, and she could afford to pick on the shorter stacks, using her chips to intimidate them.

It felt good to wear the habit again. It felt good to be accepted again, and to have the other nuns on her side, standing just beyond the barrier, cheering her on. Though she noticed Sister Bertha had wandered off, and when she'd asked, the nun was discovered in one of the side games in the other room, playing pot-limit Omaha . . .

She was winning, too.

It occurred to her that she didn't need to win. Would that be vanity, to think that she could? Would it be greed, or pride, to want to win?

She wrestled with the question without coming to an answer. And, of course, she wasn't there, yet. She figured she'd be glad to be out in any of the places left. She'd gone farther than anyone would have expected of her: a novice player, in her first big tournament. A novice player, a novice nun. The thought made her smile. On the next hand she raised aggressively with nothing from an early position, and stole the blinds.

❋

'One time,' Le Phantom said softly. He was all-in with jacks against Danny Boy's ace-queen and an ace had just come on the flop. 'One time.'

But no miracle came on the river, and Le Phantom got up, and shook everyone's hands, and then he was gone, as though he'd never been.

And then there were four.

⁂

She played tight, picking her moments, going with real hands and pushing when she did. Mikey was getting short-stacked. He kept trying to nip at Danny Boy's large stack and running into opposition. Either Danny Boy folded against Mikey's strong hands, or he called his bluff and scooped up pots Mikey couldn't afford to lose. It was coming down to an all-in but, when it came, it wasn't Danny Boy in the pot, it was the Impaler.

She hadn't seen much of Vlad's play until then. He played tighter than Mikey, and when he called Mikey's all-in, it was clear he had the advantage. Playing four-handed, you had to be looser with your starting hands. Mikey's queen-jack suited came up against Vlad's tens. It was a coin-toss gamble, the sort you had to take—she couldn't blame either of them for calling.

The flop came, then the turn, then the river. There was no jack, and there was no queen, and there was no flush. Mikey's stack was just slightly smaller than Vlad's, so when he lost, he lost everything.

'Well, I guess this is it,' he said, standing. He looked a little shaken.

Claire couldn't help feeling sorry for him. He looked so dejected, standing there, staring at the table as if he couldn't believe this was really happening to him. He'd come so close.

'You just made three hundred grand, dude,' Vlad said.

'Yeah,' Mikey said. He seemed unable to say anything more.

Danny Boy got up and shook Mikey's hand. 'It was a pleasure playing with you,' he said. He patted Mikey on the shoulder. 'I'm going to see you around, aren't I?'

'Yes,' Mikey said. 'I think so.'

'I think so too,' Danny Boy said.

Mikey shook hands with Vlad. 'You did what you had to do,' Vlad said.

'Yeah.'

Finally, it was Claire's turn.

'Good luck,' Mikey said. 'I hope you win it.'

'What will you do now?' Claire said.

'Have a drink, I think,' Mikey said, and at last he smiled. He was easy to like, she thought. She smiled too.

. . . and then there were three.

✳

From fourth to third place the prize money went up one hundred grand.

She was guaranteed at least four hundred thousand pounds now.

It was hard to even imagine that kind of money.

The difference it could make to people's lives.

But she couldn't think about the money.

Relax, her father said. It's just a game.

She smiled. For just a moment, he was there, his hand on her shoulder. The game went on. She liked playing three-handed. You didn't wait around for cards as much. You had to play loose, a weak hand in a nine-handed game was strong against just two other players. Danny Boy seemed to like seeing flops. He was an active player. Vlad had doubled up against Mikey but his stack still didn't measure up to hers or Danny Boy's. He played tighter, but they kept chipping away at his stack and he twice tried to go all-in without getting any callers, and ended up just stealing the blinds. The third time, he re-raised all-in against Danny Boy, and when he did it was one of those TV hands, as they called them, kings versus aces, and that was the end of Vlad "the Impaler" Walewski.

When Vlad was gone, they announced a short break. The stands erupted in cheers. Danny Boy smiled and shook her hand.

'Heads-up,' he said.

'My favourite,' she said.

'I'll see you in a bit, then,' he said.

'Yeah,' she said.

It was only a short break.

When it was finished, they wheeled in the money.

A million pounds in cash, just sitting on the table.

She thought it was gaudy, to be honest. She didn't want it. It was just paper, cotton paper and ink. It didn't *mean* anything. It wasn't food, or shelter, or love. It was just a fiction, no different to poker chips.

'For the last time . . . Shuffle up and deal!'

28

JACK-SEVEN. She called from the small blind. Danny Boy checked. The flop came ace-ten-deuce. She checked, Danny Boy checked. The turn was a jack. Danny Boy raised. Claire called. The river was a four. Looked like a missed flush. Danny Boy raised. Claire called.

Danny Boy showed an eight-six. Claire won the pot.

❂

Queen-six. Danny Boy raised. She called. Flop came four-three-ten, with two diamonds on board. She raised, Danny Boy folded.

❂

Two-three off on the big blind. Danny Boy raised from the small blind. Claire folded.

◉

Jack-four off. Danny Boy raised, she called. The flop came three-jack-three. She raised, Danny Boy called. The turn came a five. Check, check. An ace on the river. She raised, Danny Boy folded.

◉

Ace-eight. She raised, Danny Boy called. Nine-three-queen on the flop. Danny boy checked. She raised. Danny Boy folded.

◉

At the end of an hour they were still almost evenly matched up. Danny Boy wasn't chatting as much and Claire was in that focus point where nothing else existed but odds and cards, statistics and raises. How much to raise was almost as important as the cards you tried to represent, or what you could put your opponent on. Danny Boy liked to see flops. They played a lot of small pots, stealing blinds when they could, seeing flops, sometimes turns, sometimes rivers. It would take both of them having a big hand to make both commit all their chips into the pot. So far they had only tried to chip at each other's stacks, and when one or the other went all in, the other backed off.

There was a break and she went to see everyone. Mephistopheles materialised out of nowhere, and laughed his booming laugh when she jumped. 'Finish it, Sister,' he said. Next to him was a nice looking guy who smiled at her shyly.

'It is a good game,' he said. He had a French accent. She stared at him. 'Are you the Phantom?' she said.

He shrugged, and she laughed. He just looked like anyone else.

'We're going to hit the Seven Card Stud game,' Mephistopheles said.

'Good luck, guys.'

'Luck,' Mephistopheles said, and snorted. Then they were gone.

When she got back to the table she just sat there for a long moment. What was she trying to do? she thought. She no longer needed to win. Second place paid out six hundred thousand pounds. It was more than enough to save the convent, more money than she could have imagined. So what was she doing? Did she try to prove herself? Was she, despite it all, trying to win out of pride?'

'It doesn't matter,' she said, and laughed, surprising herself. 'It doesn't matter anymore.'

The camera stayed on her face, but she didn't notice it. She was in the small blind. She was now supposed to look at her cards.

But what was the point?

At the end of the day, she thought, you had to have faith.

She never looked at her cards. The camera hovered on her face, her hands. Claire pushed her chips across the table and said, 'All-in.'

'Call.'

The call surprised her. It was so quick. Then Danny Boy turned over his cards, and she saw why: he had pocket aces.

'She hasn't even looked at her cards, Mike!'

'Can we see what they are yet?'

'After an hour of intense heads-up poker, it looks like we're about to see the end of this Irish nun's impressive run at the EPC—oh, my!'

Claire turned over her cards. She stared at them, and had to laugh.

Seven-deuce off-suit.

It was the worst starting hand in poker.

'We're all-in for what will be the last hand of this tournament, Don, and what a heads-up this is! The best starting hand versus the worst starting hand in poker!'

'I can't believe she just . . . pushed there, Mike.'

'What was she thinking?'

'Who can tell, Mike?'

She looked across at Danny Boy. He smiled, with just a touch of anxiety. The nod he gave her was almost imperceptible. She thought he understood.

It was such a relief, to end it at last. She felt serene, surrounded by silence. The eruption of noise in the stands, the shouts and the excitement, didn't even register for her.

It was just a game, and it had been fun, but it was time, she thought, to go back to what really mattered. She hoped they'd let her back. Suddenly she missed her room, and waking up for Lauds. Missed the silence at night, and that feeling, so rare and precious, that everything was as it should be.

The dealer extracted the cards. Laid them, face down, on the felt. Flipped them up and spread them.

The flop came seven-seven-ace.

Gasps from the stands, a rueful smile from Danny Boy.

Claire had hit three of a kind.

But so had Danny Boy, and his were aces.

Her chances of winning stood at just over 4 per cent.

'*This is a hand to defy the odds, Mike—*'

'*To everyone watching at home, this is* not *how you usually play poker—*'

The dealer dealt the next card. Face down. Flipped it up.

'*Holy—!*'

The turn was a two. It gave Claire a full

house, sevens over deuces—but it gave Danny Boy a bigger full house, aces over sevens.

There was just no way she could win. Her odds were just over 2 per cent at that point. She stood up from the table. She didn't even say, 'One time.'

She wasn't even looking as the dealer dealt the final card. The river sat there, face down on the felt. She was turning away from the table when she heard the screams, felt how the whole of the Grand Hall erupted in loud noise, into which her name was woven like a refrain, 'Claire! Claire! Claire! Claire! Claire!'

'What?' she began to say. 'What?'

It was only when she turned around that she saw it: Danny Boy, standing over the table, mouth slightly open; the dealer, with a bemused look, and the tournament director, smiling, and the cameras flashing, and people running past the barriers to find her, to hold her, screaming her name, and the nuns descending down like a flock of ravens, and her mother, crying and laughing, and only then, even as she saw it, it didn't register:

The river was a seven of hearts.

She'd finished with a four-of-a-kind, sevens full.

'*What. A.* Hand! *Mike!*'

'*One could say it was the Hand of God, Don.*'

'*That's terrible, Mike.*'

'*I'm sorry, Don.*'

'*Seriously. Terrible.*'

'*I know, Don. That's what they pay me for.*'

'*You mean we get paid for this?*'

'*I don't know about you, Don . . .*'

Then she was surrounded, and Sister Bertha was holding her up in a bear hug, and Sister Mary's face was flushed with smiling, and her mother was crying, and even the Mother Superior was there.

When it had calmed down, she went and shook Danny Boy's hand. He smiled, and said, 'Congratulations.'

'Thank you.'

'I hope I get to play against you again.'

'I don't think that's very likely,' Claire said.

'That's probably for the best,' he said, laughing. 'Congratulations, again.'

'Thank you. It was . . . It was something.'

'Yes,' he said. 'Yes, it was.'

He vanished into the crowd. The cameras were on her then, and the tournament director materialised with the trophy.

'No, thank you,' she said. 'I don't need it.'

'You don't—what?'

She laughed. 'I don't need it,' she said. 'Thank you.'

She put her hands on the felt, palms down. It was the only moment that she felt a twinge of regret. The chips were still in the middle, a puddle of chips strewn this way and that. The cards were still where they'd been left. A seven-deuce, she thought. Well, that was poker for you.

A microphone, pressed on her.

'How did you do it?' the interviewer said.

The camera was on her. Claire smiled through tears.

'You just need to have a little faith,' she said.

29

'WILL YOU COME BACK with us?' the Mother
Superior said.

Claire looked down.

'I didn't think—'

'You can't be both,' the Mother Superior
said, but gently. 'But you get to choose what you
want to be in your life.'

'When I left, I'd resigned myself . . . I didn't
think I was coming back.'

'And now?'

'I don't know.'

✸

A cold wind blew through the cemetery, and
clumps of fog clung to the branches of an oak.

Somewhere in the distance she could hear a priest chanting. The ground was muddy. There were wilting flowers on the nearby graves but none by her father's tombstone.

She knelt there, by the grave. She didn't speak aloud, and her thoughts were private. She lit a candle by the grave, and the small flame struggled vainly against the wind. She cupped it in her hands and watched it strengthen, until it burned true.

❋

By the cemetery gates stood her mother and beside her stood Sister Bertha. Claire hugged her mother.

'I know,' her mother said, stroking her hair. 'I know.'

Claire took a deep breath, and then she smiled.

'Ready?' said Sister Bertha.

'I'm ready,' Claire said.

❋

No flowers on the grave, but in their stead she'd left her father a single poker chip from the casino. He would have liked that, she thought.

30

'Is it liver?' Bill Hanlon said hopefully. 'I hope it's liver.'

'It's Tuesday,' Claire said. 'Tuesday's fish and chips.'

'Fish and chips!' Bill Hanlon said. 'I love me some fish and chips, Sister.'

'I know you do, Bill,' Claire said. She looked at Bill's new leg. It was a good leg, and he moved with increasing confidence on it.

'You know my nephew,' he said. Behind him, coming through the door, was Mikey. He looked much the same as she'd last seen him in London the year before. His hair was cut more expensively, maybe. But the grin was much the same.

'Hi, Mikey.'

'Hello, Sister.'

'No-good layabout,' Bill Hanlon said; but he said it kindly.

When Bill sat down, Claire brought him a plate of fish and chips and mushy peas, and a mug of tea, and Bill thanked her. His attention turned to the food. She had never seen a man eat so whole-heartedly.

Mikey leaned on the counter.

'What brings you round to these parts?' she said.

'Come to say goodbye.'

'Oh? Are you leaving?'

'Sort of.' He smiled. 'I'm going to America.'

'You're going to enter the World Series,' she said.

'Yes. I have to, don't I.'

'Yes,' she said. 'You do.'

It was warm in the room, and filled with the smell of fish, the clink of cutlery, the chatter of voices from the television.

'You could come with me,' he said with sudden urgency. 'You could make it, you know. You could make it all the way.'

She only smiled, and then she began to fill up another plate, for Mrs Flynn who'd just come in.

'Yes,' she said. 'I know.'

LAVIE TIDHAR is the World Fantasy Award winning author of *Osama* (2011), Seiun nominated *The Violent Century* (2013), the Jerwood Fiction Uncovered Prize winning *A Man Lies Dreaming* (2014), and the Campbell Award and Neukom Prize winning *Central Station* (2016), and Locus and Campbell award nominated *Unholy Land* (2018), in addition to many other works and several other awards. His latest novels *By Force Alone* (2020) and debut children's novel *Candy* (2018 UK; as *The Candy Mafia* 2020 US). He is also the author of the comics mini-series *Adler*. New novel *The Escapement* is forthcoming in 2021, as is anthology *The Best of World SF*.

Lavie works across genres, combining detective and thriller modes with poetry, science fiction and historical and autobiographical material. His work has been compared to that of Philip K. Dick by the *Guardian* and the *Financial Times*, and to Kurt Vonnegut's by *Locus*.